The Unwritten Music Of Life

Jorge Armenteros

SPUYTEN DUYVIL
New York City

In *The Unwritten Music of Life*, music and silence divine memory. Armenteros's synesthetic maelstrom becomes both voice and metaphor. A classical composer, Nicanor, finds himself in search of missing notes. Neva, violinist/muse, may have a clue. Their languid narratives (respectively 1st and 2nd person) obliquely reveal childhood specters and their own enigmatic relationship. This is a 'large' book, a joy to read, and worthy of much contemplation. The prose is lucid and often poetic. There's mystery, animation, and quest; a right amount of magical realism, veiled eroticism, anomie and much personification. A refrain, "nothing and everything", nods to Sartre. Perhaps most salient, Armenteros, who happens to be a psychiatrist, offers an exquisitely sustained portrayal of mind. He evinces music's direct access to the unconscious. Ultimately, Neva's electrifying improvisations (like psychoanalytic free-association?) afford her a kind of peace with the past that Nicanor may then reach for.

Lauri Robertson, author of ...& *Tremolos*

Like Kieslowski's film *Blue*, Jorge Armenteros's novel *The Unwritten Music of Life* speaks directly to music's mysterious core. In the debate between absolute music, in which music can only be understood based on music itself and maintains its elegant stance in the ineffable, and program music, in which "literary" dilutions suggest that music can be paraphrased in words and translated into narrative and symbol, absolute music wins. And yet: because of listening closely to "Composition No. 33", a narrative between a composer and a violinist, between a woman, a river, Prague and Cuba, past, present and future emerges here in clear, concise elegant language. It only happens in the moment. "I am starting to think that the soul of sounds cannot be recorded." Armenteros's novel is one that rewards the closest of readings.

Leonard Schwartz, author of *Actualities*

"Music is a moral law. It gives a soul to the universe, wings to the mind, flight to the imagination, a charm to sadness, gaiety and life to everything. It is the essence of order, and leads to all that is good, just, and beautiful, of which it is the invisible, but nevertheless dazzling, passionate, and eternal form."

—Plato

Do

A melody so innocent. It cares not for the glass at the window; it passes through it. Like a child, this melody ignores its power. It goes where it fancies. It licks everything in its wake. It vibrates without knowing it. It makes no effort to assert itself, but it does. I then hear it floating in the air, a luminous, frolicking sound.

It belongs to nobody, this melody. I have tried to grab it with my hands, to hold it down in place. But this melody cannot be captured. It reverberates around me for as long as it wishes before suddenly departing. Over and over... arriving, leaving. This melody does not reside within the confines of my reality, but it has lived inside my mind for a long time.

I wonder if this is an errant melody that has forever existed. It may predate my time on this earth. If that were the case, it would likely continue to resonate once I am no longer there. I reject that harrowing thought at once, for I feel this melody is personal. That is my sentiment. But the melody cares not for how I feel. It sets the atoms in rhythmic motion when it passes by and then abandons them to their fate—to my fate.

I resolve to continue living my life, it contains enough beauty. I will first salute the sun, and later the moon. In between those two encounters, I will express myself in a visceral and pure fashion in this neoteric score challenging me. I will not allow for any other melody to infect my composition. I am inventing, going beyond the received. The only empty corner that remains in this composition is reserved for that melody, the one that refuses to linger.

Having already saluted the sun, I grab my sound recorder and head straight for the shore. The natural and shameless music of the world awaits me there. I feel emboldened today. Once I reach the shore, I come to face a wall of raw sound, deep and unrelenting. The waves, when they crest over themselves in a last suicidal effort to reach the shore, create the most thunderous reverberations. To the unversed, it is a uniform, undifferentiated sound that can be heard all along the shoreline. But that is hardly the case. Each wave roars in its own peculiar way. There are flat and sharp waves, each one crashing down from a different height. Sometimes, they moan and whimper. The wind plays them, and so does the moon. I record them and save them from oblivion for the pleasure of listening to their singular melodies, for the possibility of inserting their voices in my composition.

But the waves do not sing alone; the wind joins them, and together, they extemporize the natural music of the shore. While the waves roar, the wind howls and whistles. They do not play for a hermetic audience; they play for the universe, unbound and free. I feel their physical force deep inside my chest. And that is the force I want to capture; that is the melodic impetus I want to distill.

Sometimes the wind becomes enraged and gathers into a furious speed. It travels with desperate urgency, as if escaping death itself. In such a frenzy, the wind crashes against all standing objects: people, palm trees, pergolas, leashed dogs, sailboats… everything. It appears it has gone mad, the wind. In that incandescent state it eclipses all other sounds at the shore. It fills my sound recorder with a rumbling melody that I have yet to transpose. But that is not the mood of today's wind. It is powerful today but relatively tame.

Once I have recorded what I consider enough raw and virginal world music, I return to my apartment and sit at my studio. This mechanical portent, the sound recorder, contains in its bowels the voice of raw nature—the loose melodies, the rage, the unsung lullabies of maternal waves, the seductive whispers of the breeze, and the moaning of moist sand. All those sonic elements are now captured. What remains is for me to listen carefully to such an amalgam of voices and try to find my errant melody among them.

I listen. I listen, and I marvel at the unblemished beauty of the natural sounds. I listen some more. But to no avail. My cherished melody does not emerge. Apparently, it did not parade along the shore this morning. Or perhaps it did but refused to be captured. I wonder if this melody belongs to the natural world. Does it coalesce with the sounds of the waves and the wind? Is it shamelessly promiscuous like most other melodies? Or does this melody exist as a noble sonic entity, sliding untouched through space and time? Or even more terrifying, is this melody only a figment of my imagination?

Void of answers, I leave the loneliness of my studio behind and prepare for a full day of rehearsals at the concert hall. Music will be on trial today. My latest composition will attempt to survive the abuse of questionable playing hands. They mean well, the quartet, but my composition does not give itself so easily. It requires a gentle abandonment of accepted forms and an enthusiastic embrace of risk. Perhaps the one on trial is me and not the piece. But are we not one and the other? No, we are not. We are made of different substances. The music is ineffable, I am not.

#

I come to the concert hall because of habit and necessity, not because music resides here. Music can be found where sounds are, and sounds are everywhere in our universe—they are the ones that reveal what actually happens. In the concert hall, nothing is told anew. We come here to tell each other stories of things past. The sounds we produce inside these walls are mere reproductions of the natural music of the world. The French horn knows this very well—it thinks of itself as nothing other than a lonesome wolf. And although I have never left our earthly globe, I am confident that in sidereal space, we would hear the music of the spheres.

Mario is the first musician to greet me. I cannot tell whether he is smiling, crying, or both simultaneously. He seems agitated as much as he seems calm, but his voice is certainly convincing when he tells me the rehearsal is going as expected. I learn that the first movement is taking shape. When I ask Mario what shape that is, he gestures with his hands, tracing a circle in the air. I never thought of the first movement as being round, but round is a natural shape, so I feel encouraged.

Mario is a man who prefers not to use words. He speaks through his cello, and many times, he just remains silent. So, when I ask him if he understands the piece, he simply turns his back on me and returns to the rehearsal room. I then listen to a few cello notes floating in the air. He is responding to my question, but I cannot understand what he is trying to say. The simple melody he plays is very clear, but the mood is ambiguous, much like Mario himself.

I consider aborting the rehearsal obligation and leaving the concert hall at once. But what am I running away from? From the sound of the instruments or from the people that make those sounds? After all, the quartet is playing the music I composed. They can only interpret my success or my failure to capture the natural music of the world. They are essentially innocent. Thus, if I leave, I will be running away from myself because to listen to them is to listen to my own musical self. Or perhaps I would be running away from the disillusion of not hearing my cherished melody, the one that escapes me.

I resolve to enter the rehearsal room and confront the roundness of the first movement. The quartet seems at ease, and their playing is precise. Their approach to the composition is rather delicate, eliminating any potential angular edges. I recognize the undulation of waves and the softness of low-hanging clouds. Neva, the first violin, renders the morning mist as I had conceived it. The viola speaks like the breeze. The music feels completely natural, like the morning walk by the seashore that inspired it. But as I had expected, the fugitive melody is not there, although I remember having heard it during one of my walks. Somehow, the notes faded away and evaded my composition. I am left with a very round movement that lies in the center of an undeniable void.

I remain in a corner of the rehearsal room in complete silence, looking down at the floor and avoiding any kind of interaction. The quartet should rehearse as if I were not present, but I am very present at this moment. However, they seem to understand my desire to disappear, for the quartet continues to rehearse without stopping to address me. The second movement begins to take a triangular shape as the voices of the two violins and the cello alternate contrapuntally on equal terms. It is a less natural movement since triangles are hard to find in the wild. Still, I am delighted with their rendition. But as with the first movement, this one shows no trace of that melody. Perhaps because the melody had not taken up permanent residence inside my mind, although it feels so ancient to me, my unconscious did not wield its magic—it failed to add the ephemeral notes secretly.

Before embarking on the third movement, Neva lays

her violin on a chair and comes to the corner where I am still looking at the floor. She stands in front of me without saying a word. I am afraid she will ask for my opinion or, even worse, for instructions on how to interpret the piece. I remain still and refrain from looking at her youthful face. If I were to look at her, she might detect a sort of yearning that would alter her approach to the movement. But if this composition is the musical embodiment of that yearning, should not the musicians be aware of such nature? That is a dangerous proposition.

Neva tells me that she has attempted to play the piece in all possible ways, that she has ventured into all the silent spaces, but that she somehow gets the sensation that a few notes are missing. Neva is a fine musician but, above all, a compassionate woman. I confirm that the partition contains all the notes I meant to include and that if any are missing, I would not know where those notes are—an honest answer but pathetic, nonetheless.

They finish playing the third movement, which they execute with admirable dexterity and grace. Their interpretation blends my wishes with their natural talents, and the result is impeccable. And, naturally, they look at me in search of ratification. Still looking down at the floor, I remain silent, a behavior they will very likely interpret as arrogant and disdainful. But what do all those notes in the composition matter if the essential ones are nowhere to be found? So, I say nothing. I then leave the corner where I am standing and exit the rehearsal room. I believe Neva calls my name, "Nicanor," but I do not turn around. What matters now is to go out and join the universe where I may come across those missing notes once again.

#

Since it is too early to salute the moon, I decide to linger out on the streets and take my chances with the unknown. I do not care much for street noise, although one must admit that its cadences could be surprising. So, I direct my steps toward the park that divides this village in two. The street noises are predominantly flat to the east, whereas they tend to be rather sharp to the west. In between the two, the park acts as a mediator where most noises are natural, as would be expected given the abundance of trees, shrubs, and grasses.

People tend to gather in certain conspicuous areas of the park, primarily around fountains and at the edge of the central lake, where they must share the terrain with ducks, geese, and the dogs that chase them. People introduce the human buzz, a white and graceless sound that clobbers the harmonics of leaves touching each other and fluttering in the wind. It is necessary to escape them, the people, and find those corners in the park where natural sounds are unmolested. So that is precisely what I do by taking a narrow path leading to a small clearing open to the sky—a calm and tranquil place void of people. I lie on my back over the minty grass and spread my arms and legs. I am open to the sound of the trees, to their musing.

As I try to concentrate on the sonic material around me, my heart, a steady and resounding drum beating at 72 beats per minute, introduces a profound and thunderous basso continuo that drowns the natural sound of the trees. My ears do not capture this sound outside my body; they seem to register it directly from within myself. But I did not come here to listen to my internal organs; I came here in search of nature's melody. My body, however, interferes and asserts its materiality, perhaps reminding me that I am not a separate entity in this universe. I am just another note.

When I try to remember the first time I heard my cherished melody, my memory fails to identify a particular time or place. Even when I make a strong effort to ascertain its origin, I end up with uncertainty, perhaps because uncertainty is ubiquitous in our lives or perhaps because my mind is trying to protect me from some unsavory memories.

There, there I am, proud of myself, a revolutionary cadet the teacher says, ready to sing "The Internationale." At home I'm told I can sing anything I want, but not that song. That put an end to my days in school. I'm not allowed to go anymore— no more friends after that. And there I am again, little, playing alone, not singing. But it doesn't matter because I'm leaving to a place where there's candy. It's far they tell me. Then again, I see myself in a corner, waiting, for the plane, for kids to play with, for candy.

Regardless of the actual mechanism, I am ignorant of

the genesis of the melody. Did it soothe me during my innocent days in the crib, or did it arrive later when I started yearning for eternity as a young man? It could also have seduced me when music installed itself in the core of my creative self. That mystery embellishes the melody with an irresistible allure that makes me behave in strange ways, like lying on the grass with my eyes closed while listening to the drumming of my heart.

As I continue to lie supine and open, my heart rate eventually slows down and settles at a comfortable rate of 60 beats per minute—a tempo that reminds me of Satie's Gymnopédie No. 2 with its inherent complacency and atmospheric acceptance. I then begin to ignore my body, to become deaf to the sound of the machine. Then, the aural presence of the grass, the trees, the clouds, and the winds that come to visit grows. Each of those natural elements plays the fundamental notes of their atoms. But they have always played their music together, an ensemble as beautiful as it is naïve, thus, eternal.

This natural symphony has no beginning, for it lacks a primordial silence before the first note. It has no composer, for the natural elements arrange themselves as they wish. And no director can tell the elements what their pitch should be nor what tempo to follow. The music simply happens, unencumbered, ethereal. And it is within this symphony that I search for passages resembling the melody I am looking for—perhaps a few notes, a short phrase, a suggested rhythm—anything.

As I listen, as I listen some more, marveling at the creative impetus of the natural world, my hopes begin to fade once again when no melody materializes. I may have arrived early, or late, at the performance. Or this may not be the stage where the melody is being played. Or the melody does not want to be heard, afraid that I would attempt to capture it. I do my best to comprehend, but I am defeated.

A disturbing thought then enters my mind, distracting me from the act of listening. Without wanting, I begin to consider the idea that there is not one melody but multiple ones. Perhaps what I hear are random accumulations of notes which I construe as a single melody and bestow it with a uniqueness it does not have. Another unsettling thought is that I may just be chiseling a melody out of syncopated city noises, like a sculptor releasing form out of a piece of rock. If such were the case, I would have already composed the melody, and it would reside within the confines of my physical reality. But I am sure that is not true because my original compositions are neither beautiful nor sublime.

Daylight begins to weaken, a sign that I have been lying on my back for a while. It is better to stop listening, to stop considering obtuse thoughts that threaten to shift my center. So, I get up on my feet and start walking through the park. The crowds are still gathering in their preferred places, and their buzz continues to disturb the natural harmonics of the universe. I try not to listen and accelerate my pace. The saccadic rhythm of my steps eventually delivers me to my studio, where loneliness is naturally awaiting me. Instinctively, I sit at the piano as if I were to work on a composition, ready to create a beautiful and sublime sound. But before I play a single note, I step up to the window. And noticing that it has already shown its face, I salute the moon.

RE

Considering the way in which she plays the violin, I am certain the violin likes to be played by her. Neva seems to unearth the sentiments buried under the sheet music; she digs them out with her bow without violence. No, there is no violence, only a gentle persuasion. I would also like to be played by her. She could elicit some of those notes hidden deep inside my composer's carapace… but I am not a violin.

She said notes were missing from my composition. That means she has attempted to drink from the emotional rivers that flow among the five horizontal lines and found them dry. I do not know what notes she is referring to, and I am not certain what emotions they could engender. Is she implying that I am somehow emotionally crippled? Perhaps she does not care about my shortcomings and is simply trying to understand the emotional depth of the score. Could she be trying to play me?

I wrote Composition No. 33 hoping to affect the listener, to make them feel as if they were banished into forests far away, to make them linger suspended over the plasma of an early universe. I thought all the emotions would be accessible once the bow struck the strings. But Neva seems to detect that those forests, although far away, are rather lonesome because their voices cannot be heard. Those missing notes are the ones suspended, frozen, unassailable.

However sensitive Neva may be, she knows very little

about me, so she could not construe an explanation for the missing notes. All she can detect is that the piece is not complete. The composition, however, stands as a complete piece on its own. The fact that a perceptive individual notices a certain emotional void does not destroy the merits of the piece if it were to contain any. I better stop this thought process. Why should I doubt my capacity as a composer? Or maybe I should. If I fail to express the emotional depth of the universe by means of musical notes, would that not make me a lesser composer? I cannot answer that question.

I could ask Neva to reveal the notes she feels are missing. I could tell her to play them on her violin. She is more than capable of playing any notes and conveying any meaning with her bow and strings. Of course, her interpretation would be speculative since neither of us knows what those notes are, but just as well. Perhaps, while listening to her proposition, I may get a glimpse of the fugitive melody. If her playing touches on some underground sentiment that somehow escapes me, I would be closer to understanding why the melody does not want to keep me company.

#

There is no time to waste. After my sun salutation, I prepare to return to the concert hall in the morning. The quartet likes to warm up before tackling a new piece. And they refuse to play in front of me until they have rehearsed the entire composition at least once. So, when I stand at the door of the rehearsal room with an eager expression on my face, they do not seem ecstatic to see me.

Mario says that they have not started yet and that the instruments and their hands are cold. I am shivering as he is, but not because of the frigid temperature in this decrepit concert hall, but because I am afraid of what Neva may play if I ask her. Furthermore, since I cannot ask her to play anything different from Composition No. 33 until they are finished rehearsing, I will rest shivering for a while. This time, however, I will not hide in a corner and look down at the floor. I will stand right in front of the quartet and absorb their performance.

So here I stand, impervious but frightened. The first movement begins to take the round shape Mario had previously described. A few false notes confirm that the players are indeed cold. But they do not seem to care about those notes, neither do they care that I am invading their space so early in the rehearsal. They cannot be judged at this time, and they know it.

Once they embark on the second movement, I notice that Neva has stopped looking at the score and instead focuses on me. Her notes fill the room, but I do not hear them. All I sense is the intensity of her gaze bearing down on me. I feel as if she is imploring, asking for the totality of the notes and emotions. But I have nothing to offer. So, I divert her plea by looking down at the floor once more.

As I listen to the quartet interpreting my music, I get the sense that I am talking to myself. It feels as if my voice is trying to say something, but I cannot understand what that is. Notes and silences interweave with each other trying to utter meaningful phrases. Music happens and harmonic sequences fly around the room, but I cannot fathom what I am trying the tell myself. I considered Composition No. 33 to be a complete piece; however, it had not been played by Neva yet. She now makes it evident that my score is not speaking clearly.

When the third movement begins, my eyes are still focused on the wooden parquet lining the floor. Neva may still be gazing at me in hopes for an emotional explanation. But, no, no… I cannot bear to look up. What could I say to her, to myself? Better to let the music continue until it exhausts itself. Only then, under the cloak of silence, would I be able to put into words my insecurities. If, of course, I have the courage to do so.

Once the final harmonies dematerialize, the rehearsal room returns to its mundane existence as a place where dreams are sometimes realized, and other times shattered. I am afraid this time the results are of the later sort. What ensues, however, is silence. A silence begging for interruption because it feels tense, uneasy. None of the musicians say a word. Instead, they look at me expecting that I would criticize their interpretation. I, who am no longer certain about the meaning of my work nor about its deficiencies.

Neva sustains her gaze. It burns me. For a moment I detect a slight twitch of her lower lip and think she is ready to speak. But she does not say a word. I wonder what she is really thinking. I also wonder what the other three are thinking. Mario's expression seems neutral, neither ecstatic nor sullen. Leandro, being the second violin that he is, seems to be waiting for Neva to open the discussion. As for Sandra, who cannot stop fidgeting with her viola, her face seems to glow with satisfaction. Only a quartet like this one, comprised of such diverse creatures, could interpret Composition No. 33, and come to a dead silence at the end. Perhaps the problem is my presence. Here I am, a composer who attends a rehearsal of his own music and stands in dejected silence looking down at the floor. How are they supposed to react to the music, to my presence? This time I am not turning my back on discomfort. I will be candid and reveal my insecurities. I will withstand Neva's questions and comments. I am not running away from this concert hall. So, I speak...

Why did I write this music? I have no clear ideas; I do not even have ideas. There are tugs, impulses, blocks, and everything is looking for a form; the rhythm moves into play, and I write within that rhythm. I write by it, moved by it, and not by that thing they call thought, which turns out melodies, concerts, or what have you. Then comes the moment when what I write seems complete, and that is when I stop. Sometimes I recognize the melodies I excluded from the composition, the abandoned ones. Other times, those melodies are unknown to me.

After speaking those words, I lower my head and explore the geometry of the wooden parquet which appears so at ease in its angular symmetry, so content under its coat of warm and golden varnish, so in peace with itself. I wait for and expect a response from any of the four musicians. Nonetheless, nobody says a word. Silence is only the preamble from which musical notes or words emerge. From this silence, however, nothing seems to grow. Seconds, minutes, or centuries pass by, I am not sure, but the silence remains intact. Nevertheless, I am not running away. No, I am staying inside this silence.

Then I hear it again. The innocent melody floating in the air with its luminous, frolicking sound. I identify it at once—the fugitive, the errant. With utmost caution I lift my head and regard the quartet. Everyone is standing quietly looking at me apart from Neva, whose chin firmly presses her violin's body while her right arm gently bows the strings. What she is playing is a mystery to me; what I hear is the innocent melody in all its irreverent grace. I marvel at this miracle but fail to understand it. An impossibility this is, how could Neva improvise the melody I fail to seize?

She then stops playing altogether and once again looks at me with those intense eyes demanding an explanation I do not possess. I could tell her that I knew exactly what she was playing, but that would be a lie. I could ask her to tell me how she came about that melody, but that may be dangerous. I could also ignore what just happened, but that would be miserable for me. So, I only manage to ask a simple question. I ask Neva if she is content with her interpretation of Composition No. 33. She responds by saying that she is essentially satisfied but that her fingers keep finding notes that are not written in the score and that she must somehow release those notes.

I do not know what to say. And that is precisely what I do—I say nothing. I turn my back on the quartet and leave the rehearsal room dragging the silence with me. I make my way out of the concert hall and enter the outside world where the natural sounds immediately engulf me. The silence, now, is inside of me.

Mi

What is the point of writing down the notes? So that a capable musician can interpret the thoughts and emotions that crossed my mind at the time of composition? What about the notes I choose not to include? They are plentiful and just as eloquent. Perhaps I am lying to myself when I deem a composition finished. At that moment a great number of reductionist choices have been already made. Yes, the essence of the composition is distilled but at the cost of excluding legions of viable melodies. There is nothing final about that finished piece since it constitutes a reduced musical universe that begs for expansion. What a meager exercise!

On the other hand, I could convince myself that by selecting a group of notes and arranging them as a composed piece, I would be exalting them, allowing them to shine and express feelings they would not otherwise be capable of. In that case, I would not be composing anything, I would just be editing. And who am I to edit the universe of sounds? And why should an audience care for my condensation of such a vast universe?

What do I hear when I wake up in the morning? Is it noise or is it music? Is it the sound of the earth turning or the voices of memories? Yes, as in many other mornings, when I wake up, I unveil my senses. But how could I write the music of the morning if, indeed, those sounds are perhaps mere sensations. And with only twelve notes at my disposal, I would be a fool to embark on such a task. So, again, what is the point of writing down musical notes?

Since the path I follow offers no answers, I decide to change direction and head for the unknown. I should venture into the world of unwritten music, loose tunes, arbitrary arrangements, aleatory melodies, and improvised performances. In essence, I should look for the risk inherent in extemporaneous performances. There are places where such music is performed, I am aware, but I shun them because they exist outside of the canon. But whose canon? The one I am trying to join by writing the expected? Clearly, by writing the expected, even if I think I excel in my compositions, I fail. Something goes missing—a melody, an emotion.

I prepare to travel through the night until I find a venue where the relationship between order and disorder is being explored. I leave the solitude and silence of my apartment and take to the streets. The old town is my best bet since that is where irreverent things happen. For something to grow anew, it needs to feed on the decomposed fabric of old elements. For something to shine, it needs darkness. And through darkness, I advance until arriving at *The Cave of the Forgotten*, a place I have never visited because of its name, a jazz club of sorts.

Being a cave, the only way to enter the club is by descending a set of stairs from where a warm and tired air emanates. I listen for musical notes and hints of what awaits me, but I hear only chatter and laughter and the clinking of glasses. A man and a woman come up the stairs wearing the faces of the forgotten: eyes semi-closed, a smirk hanging from the side of their mouths, and an air of not being here but not being anywhere else either. Perhaps when we are forgotten by the world, we only exist for ourselves in a state of subdued bliss.

As I begin my descent into this forgotten world, the musicians begin to play, and the chatter and laughter quickly dissipate. I cannot see who is playing, but I can hear the instruments' voices. There is a piano playing short and sustained chordal and melodic fragments. There are the overtones of a saxophone. There is the sharp attack on cymbals and a resonant bass drum. And, to my surprise, the phrasing of a violin. I cannot recognize the music, a powerful exposition of multiple harmonic ideas, an unwritten fabric of sounds reverberating inside the crowded space. Looking for safety and order, I find an open seat in a corner away from the stage and install myself among the shadows. I then follow the notes to their source: the chords to the pianist, the hoarseness to the sax player, the crashing cymbals to the drummer, and the violin phrasing to no other than Neva herself, who stands in the center of the stage as if standing in the center of the universe. Neva, Neva, who are you?

Her violin speaks in a voice different from the one I am used to hearing in the concert hall. This is not Neva, the interpreter of my compositions; this is Neva unbound. She seems to be exploring, inventing, and expressing love and fear. She is not looking for notes since the notes give the impression of coming from inside herself. She seems to be playing herself out. The other players respond to her voice; they validate, sometimes antagonize, or accentuate, but ultimately merge with her improvised playing, creating a composition that could never be written.

The ensemble continues to play one piece after another. Or perhaps it is all a single piece mutating over time where freedom and spontaneity are on display. Are these individual musical ideas weaved together, or are these interactive commentaries, each within its own flesh? I wonder what the constraints are in this kind of music. But more important, what are the risks?

The risk for me is to be noticed by Neva. If she were to spot me in the audience, her playing might change and loose spontaneity. Or is that a grandiose sense of myself, to consider that my condition as a composer weighs heavily on how musicians play? She may not care for what I think—she has confronted me with her own thinking already. She said that she plays the notes that need to be played. In that case, what she is now playing is her own imperative, and my presence would be of no consequence. But since I cannot be sure, I remain in this shadowy corner where the music comes to meet me. I hide, and I listen.

After a very inspired solo by the sax player, Neva embarks on a journey that confirms to me the undeniable role of the violin in improvisational jazz. She seems to go beyond rituals, structured harmony, melody, or rhythm— she soars. She plays those notes, the necessary ones, with urgency and conviction. I am not sure that she is playing for the audience. I sense that she is playing for herself, to satisfy a yearning that only she can feel. And the audience seems to comprehend for they respond with encouraging applause.

She then stops abruptly, and so do the other instruments. A silence begins to grow slowly and installs itself in the center of the cave. Everyone senses its weight, a moist silence perfumed by cigarette smoke and the smell of alcohol. It grows so heavy that it begs to break into pieces and release all the tensions: the musical tension, the perspiring tensions, the tension of bottled anger, and that of bubbling smiles. But nobody in the audience moves, and neither do the musicians. We are all together in this sunken cathedral, forgotten, witnessing a small miracle we cannot understand. And after some unfathomable time, Neva lifts her violin and begins to play again. In the beginning, she moves around the notes with caution, feeling them as if discovering a new territory. Then, she releases one phrase after another until a precise melody takes shape. It bounces from wall to wall and enters deep into my consciousness. I recognize it at once, the innocent melody that escapes me. I feel it burning me, speaking to me. But by the time I try to hold on to it, Neva has stopped playing, and the piano is now taking its solo.

I wonder if Neva is aware of what she just played. Is she deliberately playing the agglomeration of notes at the right tempo to render my fugitive melody recognizable? Or is the melody bypassing her conscious intention, making its way through her fingers, and finally taking shape as sound vibrations? I cannot tell from the shadows of this corner what has happened. It seems to me that she was improvising, playing extemporaneously. That melody is not written down. No, she does not need a score; her sensitivity provides all the necessary notes.

The ensemble continues to delight the audience with their imaginative playing. Everyone seems happy not to know what will be heard next. And the musicians themselves seem to marvel at their own spontaneous discoveries. When the night comes to an end, the instruments put away, the drinks finished, the room saturated with smoke, the hearts pulsating, nobody will remember what was played. Satisfied, people start departing, arising from the depths of the cave. I wait in the shadows until Neva takes her violin and leaves through the door. She never saw me. I think I saw her. I think I heard the innocent melody. But it does not matter. I must leave this cave now. Everything and everyone will be forgotten.

FA

You played well. You are convinced because the audience responded with enthusiasm to every one of your solos. The images that come to your mind are clear: applause, head nodding in acceptance, glasses clinking, alcohol swirling down people's throats. Then there were the fellow musicians who seemed ignited by your solos and played with verve and abandon. You would have played for another hour, but they needed to close the club. They must obey orders.

Your violin felt at ease tonight. In times like this you think the wooden box reads your mind. Or perhaps, your mind is a sort of violin. A kindred spirit, you have a sensation, and the violin plays the appropriate notes. Or a few notes come to your mind and the violin provides the sensation. It may go both ways. The truth is that you have no need to guide your violin, it knows how to sing on its own. Sometimes, when you are not sure what you are thinking about, the violin takes over and interprets your uncertainty. That is exactly what happened tonight. You played melodies and phrases you have never heard before. The violin must have sensed those subterranean harmonies, like a dog sniffing for truffles, and upon encountering them, dug them out. You do not remember what you played, but it felt good to have played whatever that was.

Every time you exit from *The Cave of the Forgotten* it feels as if you die a little. There is so much energy, so much life gets transacted inside the cavernous space that the outside world, with all its predetermined rules and regulations, seems like a deaden place. Your life straddles both spaces, but you know where life tickles you best. Tomorrow at the concert hall you will be Neva again—the expected one. You will interpret the sheet music with precision. You will lend out your artistry to the imagination of another person. You will be a vehicle. You will not let the violin run amok with its own ideas. Reign it in, control it. Every note needs to be accounted for, every feeling. Composition No. 33 is not your personal music, and you know that. So, you will make it shine with the prescribed emotions, even if they are not your own emotions. It does not matter since you are only a conduit. And if something is missing, as you felt during the previous rehearsal, you will stay quiet—if you can.

The night overtakes you; it takes you inside its breast, where nothing is expected from you. This night, so quiet, brings you to your small apartment where you cannot practice because of the neighbors. They do not care if the music you play is yours or someone else's. They just do not want to hear your violin. They do not want to see you either, for they lower their eyes and ignore you when you cross them in the lobby. You do not know what kind of people they are, but you live among them.

Despite your overcoming tiredness, you decide to look at the score of Composition No. 33 in search of suspicious silences where unwritten notes could be hidden. You wonder what forces led to the creation of the piece; what thoughts populated Nicanor's mind during its composition. You try to distill the emotional drive behind the piece, but no single feeling dominates. The more you try to open the heart of the piece, the more it closes. It is a musically challenging piece and holds itself well against the canon and other contemporary pieces. But there is something that is not there, and you cannot ascertain what that is. It appears as if the true composition hides behind the notes. There seems to be a music behind the music, a phantom score that you cannot play because the notes have fallen away. But these are your speculations only. Mario has not mentioned anything to you nor has Sandra. You could be constructing an imaginary scenario where non-existent notes express the absent emotional content from the tangible score of Composition No. 33.

As your eyes scour the staves, the music comes alive in your mind. The passages take shape, the rhythm asserts itself, and you clearly hear your violin among the other instruments. Your mind, not your violin, is interpreting the score in its entirety—from beginning to end and from the end to the beginning. No vacuums, no dead alleys, no mysterious absences. The notes are the notes, and the feelings are the feelings. What your mind interprets is what is written on the page. So, you wonder what was missing the last time you played the composition. Why did it seem to you that notes were missing or that feelings might have been absconded? Maybe you are tired now, and possibly your musical self does not want to respond to music written by others. Or perhaps there is too much reality seeping into your mind. You fall asleep and that is the end of it.

The morning surprises you with its stealthy arrival. When you open your eyes, the morning has already installed itself in your bedroom. It seems to be looking at you, waiting for your entrance into the reality of the day. In the absence of shadows, everything becomes evident, and reality becomes harsher. Nighttime also contains reality, but it seems kinder and softer to you. However, the morning is in front of you, and you cannot deny its presence. You will proceed through the day, through the rehearsals, and through your life.

Once the passage of time has settled your mind and ushered in the imminent reality of the day, you open the violin case and awaken your friend from its stupor. The violin offers itself to you and asks no questions. It seems at peace with itself, content even. At the onset, you refrain from playing a single note, you just listen to the natural sound of its wooden body. You bring your ears next to the f-holes and wait for a melody to emerge, any melody. But all you hear is the passage of air through the body of the violin, no resonance, no arranged set of notes. It does not assert its presence. Just as you are doing, the violin is waiting for the reality of the day to come forth.

As you both contemplate the blossoming of the day, you regard your violin and attempt to decipher its intentions. It seems like your violin prefers to play unadulterated music, the one that arises from genuine feelings, that expresses itself for no other reason than an original imperative to exist. If the music shows any sings of undue manipulation, your violin will still play it, but it may take the liberty to modify the score. Sometimes it suppresses notes, while other times it infuses the score with buried feelings. You respect your violin and allow it to exist as the instrument it is. As a result, your interpretations are sometimes peculiar. This is more often the case during daytime when you perform the music of others. At nighttime, when you join the forgotten ones, you and your violin are free from expectations and the music you both create owes nothing to anyone.

But this is still daytime, and your duty is to arrive at the concert hall where the last rehearsal of Composition No. 33 will take place. You do not need the sheet music at all, you know every single note by heart. So, you are not concerned with memory lapses. You are also comfortable with your interpretation, your articulation, your bow strokes. You know the dynamic fluctuations of the piece; where to play softly and where to enhance the sound. You comprehend the entirety of the composition. What you cannot foresee is how your violin will react today. And even more questionable, whether buried feelings will, once again, impose themselves musically.

Time continues to ooze, drop by drop. But you are in no hurry to set foot in the concert hall. You do not want to be the first to arrive, for that will force you to wait. And while waiting, your violin may become restless and start concocting ideas. Better to arrive a little late, after everyone has settled and they have started wondering where you are. That will also reduce the time before the start of the rehearsal when the others could ask what you were doing last night. They do not know about *The Cave of the Forgotten*, and you prefer to keep it that way. That part of your personal world is in direct opposition to the part that occupies you in the daytime. You know they are compatible, that they feed from each other. But some musicians may think of you as illegitimate, an impure and prostituted violinist.

After the last drop, once time has exhausted itself, you make your entrance into the rehearsal room where Mario is playing a few sullen notes on his cello. With no time for small talk, you take your place, bring your violin to your chin, and gesture that you are ready to start playing. The first movement begins, and you brace yourself, for you do not know where the violin will take you.

#

You decide to create a vacuum, a space without air where sound waves fail to advance. And you will place yourself in the center of that vacuum hoping to hear nothing but silence. This is not an escape, for you are not being persecuted, but a parenthesis, a moment to exist as a simple person and not as a violinist. When your ears are engaged, music is everywhere, it infuses your world day and night. Everything gets transformed into harmonies, even the color of the grass in the park. With a few exceptions, those harmonies are pleasurable, and you let them caress your body. The horrendous ones, the ones that lie, you push aside and castigate them into oblivion. But occasionally you crave that vacuum where you have no obligation to make choices.

For the moment the silence is genuine, clean, even beautiful. In this silent universe you are not necessarily happy, but not morose either. You are just yourself—unattached to melodies and the emotions they evoke. Sometimes, when inhabiting this silent universe, you wonder if music really matters, if it is necessary to allow your auditory sense to determine a mood, a feeling. And what is a feeling after all? A derivative emotion brought about by your sensorial organs? What if you had no organs? You know you have sensorial organs and for that reason alone you put aside this line of thought.

While under the dome of silence, in the absence of music, you reconsider your condition as a violinist. Is it a condition, or a profession? You profess to play as best as you can. Would that make it a devotion? You are devoted to playing honestly. But are you being honest when you play notes not found in the score? For example, if a melody inserts itself into your consciousness and makes its way through your fingers as they move up and down the neck of the violin and make the bow oscillate, are you being true to the written music or to your emotional self instead? Assuming that you are true to yourself, can any interpretation then be correct morally? If your fingers play what is written by the composer but your emotional self intervenes in ways not predicted by the composer, are you being dishonest?

The answer to that question is a mystery, one you will not try to unravel while you enjoy existing in the center of this vacuum where you are free not to answer the questions that arise and where making choices is optional. There is only silence. Your thoughts, although incisive and penetrating, are essentially silent. And you would have preferred to remain in this placid state of mind. However, somehow, an unannounced melody pierces the veil of silence and reaches your tympanic membranes, your cochlear ducts, your brain, and, therefore, your emotional self.

Since silence is what surrounds you at this moment, you know this melody is probably coming from inside yourself. These cannot be sound waves carried by the wind, these are notes emanating from that white center of yours. It is a simple melody, seemingly benign, one you have no recollection of having played before. It behaves like a butterfly, following an erratic path and stumbling from note to note as it floats in the center of the silent vacuum. It engenders no memories, this melody, but it gives you a sense of ease, like an old friend or like the taste of strawberries.

You try to sing along, to imitate the sound of the melody, but your voice cannot be heard because the vacuum sequesters all sounds; your vocal rendition produces only muteness. The melody sings itself; it does not need you, it just goes through you, beyond you, without leaving any traces of its passage. And once the butterfly melody flies away, all that it leaves behind is a sensation of naturalness within you but not a single musical note.

Inebriated by the tranquility of the moment and hoping for a reencounter with the melody, you step out of the vacuum and fetch your violin. You bring it to your chin and start digging into the strings with the Mongol hair. You play nothing and everything, allowing for the notes to array themselves in whatever way they see fit. You put aside your musical intentions and invite your white center to express itself again. The sound of the violin fills the room, harmonies, phrases, a music of sorts. What is clear is that the melody has vanished, and when you try to recreate it in your playing, all you come up with are random notes.

Do not blame the violin since it has nothing to do with it. The violin has not altered or reconfigured what you were just playing. It is only operating as a conduit this time, transmitting an acoustic version of your thoughts and emotions. You regard it with indignant eyes for not playing the sound that traversed your mind a few minutes ago. But, no, the violin does not play the melody because the melody has abandoned you, it is no longer within the white center of yours.

#

It does not matter what music you play. It makes no difference if the composer is dead or alive. If you are interpreting the musical ideas of others, you are not creating anything new or distinctive. Yes, there are nuances in the way you interpret a piece. You could impart a personal touch to the composition and make it shine. The audience even marvels at your artistry, at your virtuosity. But virtuosity is nothing other than a well-honed skill, one that makes average mortals salivate. Seemingly out of reach, virtuosity captures people's imaginations and draws their applause. But what are they celebrating, your dexterity or the composer who wrote the piece?

To create something completely unique you need to return to the white center of yours. That inner space without musical responsibilities where the essence of you resides. Only from within that space can you create the music that belongs to you, to your cells and neural connections. The music that responds to your personal history, that emerges from your fears and dreams. However, that inner space is perfectly shot when you play for the quartet. It becomes unassailable the moment you start playing the notes in the sheet music. You join the other musicians and, together now, all of you join the composer. And in so doing, you lose yourself.

There are times, and this frightens you, when you reach deep into your core and come up empty-handed. This has occurred on several occasions while playing a solo. While flying high, attempting to connect one musical phrase with another, you have missed your step, fallen to the ground, and crashed. Bruised and dubitative, your confidence looks at you with disdain. Those blunders matter little to *The Cave of the Forgotten* crowd because nobody remembers anything afterward. But they leave an imprint on you, they make you feel vulnerable. Then you start wondering if you are talented enough to invent on the fly, to ascend like a lark through the thin improvisational air. What saves you from the corrosive grip of doubt is the next solo—when you often recapture your form, your inner sound, your very own music.

#

The clock in the railway platform insists on showing its intrusive face. It tells you the train should enter the station within five minutes. But you know that is a lie. The train is late; that is the only truth that matters. The train is late, and you will be late. By the time you arrive at the shore, the seagulls would have already forgotten about you. The world is impatient, it will not wait for you.

You go to the shore because the shore will not come to you. When searching for openness and freedom, your apartment and the concert hall provide you with walls and frontiers. There is always the mind, inside of which you can hide. But sometimes, the mind needs external confirmation of its boundless nature. You also go to the shore because of the colors. Blue makes you feel expansive, as if you were an ocean yourself. Then there are the seagulls with their frenetic activity and their shameless cacophonies. They do not sing in unison, and they do not care.

When the train arrives at the station you are quick to

get into the car and sit by the window. Soon enough the train departs and from this side of the windowpane you watch as the world outside begins to pass you by. You are centered, focused, and steady. The outer world is the one moving. And every tree becomes a note, and every house an arpeggio, until the speed of the world increases creating a continuous hum that will carry you all the way to the final station where the shore awaits you.

The train goes and goes until the air becomes impregnated with saltpeter, then it stops. When you descend from the car, your first impulse is to run to the edge of the sea at once. That is where the openness you yearn for lingers, where the seagulls gambol. But you decide to restrain your impetus and regard the boundless space from afar. Even if you are late, you will be early, for your inner music can only be played when you are ready. So, you compose yourself, empty your mind from remnants of melodies past, and begin to walk toward the sea at your slow personal rhythm. The march of your steps, an adagio at ease with yourself, brings you through the sands to the edge of the white surf where you stand and look far into the horizon.

The only sound you hear is that of your memories. They seem to emerge from behind the blue horizon line and swagger their way toward you. They begin as insignificant lullabies, but as they get closer, they acquire a more nuanced structure that you hear with pristine clarity. They sing your story, the pleasant and the horrible moments. One song talks about the times of loneliness, another about your early bouts of ambition, and another about your constant fear of failure. These are the songs of your life, swirling around you, making sure that you know who you really are. That is how it always happens. All exiles are drawn to the sea, and you are no exception. You left your land to come to this land. And when you regard the horizon, everything that already happened rushes into your mind as music from the past.

Once the wave of past songs rolls over you, a magnificent silence takes hold. Content with being who you are, your mind opens a seance of reflection. The first consideration pertains to your condition as a violinist. Your father, that monster you abhor, chose the instrument because he wanted to be a violinist himself and failed. You were younger and more talented, he thought. So, he sent you away to perfect the violin and to make a living playing it. Perhaps you would have chosen to play the violin yourself but that was not an option then. But it is an option now. You can continue as a professional or put the violin to sleep forever. You can play the music written by others or only play what comes from within. At the same time, you can decide not to decide and simply contemplate the immensity of the sea while listening to the songs of your memories.

A great black-backed gull interrupts your meditations by crisscrossing the horizon line. After two or three graceful maneuvers, it lands right in front of you. Although the size of the bird intimidates you, especially its powerful bill, its pale yellow eyes hold the softness of a vulnerable creature. The gull expects nothing from you; it simply marvels at your presence. And you marvel as well, for no wildlife ever comes this close to you. You regard each other in peace as if the encounter had been prearranged by nature itself. There is no use in talking to the gull, for it will not comprehend, but there is always music to share. So, you start to vocalize a simple melody, abandoning it to the whims of the wind, the notes yearning to stay up there in the sky like air transformed into clouds.

The gull flutters its wings slightly and shifts its weight from one leg to the other while sustaining its gaze on you. Your music must have an effect, there is no doubt. The bird could have attacked you or flown away disinterested. Instead, it remains in front of you as attentive as any audience you ever had. You share the same place in the sand, and you are both alone this moment. Your song is your call, one the gull has probably never heard. Does it elicit memories of waves past, of turbulent winds, of fallen companions? You will never know.

At the end of your song the silence installs itself once more. You barely hear the surf as it crawls over the sand. Your memories have fallen silent. This moment should last forever, but that is simply impossible. And the gull seems to comprehend that reality for it pushes hard with its legs and starts flapping its enormous wings. Once it has gained altitude, the gull emits a deep laughing cry that ruptures the silence. You know that call is meant for you.

You return to the realm of your thoughts, knowing that

there is always a link in what appears to be a fragmented universe of disparate minds and intentions. The link is music. It does not matter what music or what instrument, but music. Your memories speak to you through music, nature speaks to you through music. So, it is within that domain that you should search for answers. Thus, considering the violin once more, whether you play Nicanor's composition or the thing they call jazz may be of no consequence— contrary to what you have previously believed. Written notes are not more solid than those which arise from the white center of yours. The audience will absorb both kinds of sounds equally and will be variously affected based on individual taste. In either case, you would have provided the necessary link bridging the multiple sensibilities. What essentially matters is to make the violin sing.

So, you decide not to decide, for there is no need to do so. The rehearsal room will be waiting for you. Composition No. 33 will be mastered. At *The Cave of the Forgotten,* you will explore your intimate voice. The violin will respond to your caress and sing on your behalf. And if it happens that unannounced melodies manage to circumvent the filter of the expected, you will welcome and foster them as you would a cherished memory or a laughing gull.

Sol

The more I try to forget the more I remember. Purposeful forgetting does nothing other than carving deeper cuts into the delicate membrane of our memories. Those grooves remain: her playing, her looseness, her unencumbered agility. Every note new and raw and chance. Never repeated. How could I forget that Neva? Why should I try to forget that Neva? If I were to touch that image, would it disintegrate? Maybe it should be left unmolested, free in its sub-cellar existence.

Five days is all I have before the concert. One more rehearsal. And then what happens? Would the melody continue to cross my path? Would Composition No. 33 survive the critics' onslaught? Would I be capable of writing music in the way I used to? Does any of this matter? I am not certain, and for that reason I need to act. Let uncertainty paralyze me not.

What I know about Neva amounts to very little. I do not know how she joined the quartet, what conservatory she attended, why is she drawn to improvisation, what places she frequents, is she alone in the world, is she sentimental, does she know things about me that I do not know myself? She is certainly a symphony, but I do not know the notes that compose her. Thus, what I hear are deformed echoes of her.

My first inclination is to call Mario and casually inquire about Neva. He would have some concrete information as to her origins and whereabouts. But what would he know about her desires, her secrets? Probably not very much, and even if he had a minimal idea, he would be too ambiguous to answer in a straight fashion. I am not calling Mario. Instead, I could improvise my approach to her. I could venture out to the vicinity of those places she must visit—like the concert hall, or even *The Cave of the Forgotten*—and hope for a seemingly chance encounter. Yes, I would be facilitating the meeting, but the consequences would be completely unexpected. Every note new and raw and chance.

Armed… No, not armed; I should say "equipped." Equipped with my sound recorder tucked into a briefcase, I erupt from my apartment, hoping to confront the unforeseen. As this is still daytime, the logical choice is to hover around the concert hall and try my luck. If I were to fail in my daytime attempt, there is always nighttime awaiting. Nighttime is always there, at the end. But for the moment, I walk toward the angular streets surrounding the concert hall. The concert hall is nothing but a box with no aesthetic attributes, which finds itself in the middle of a non-distinct neighborhood where streets cut each other in frightening angles.

On the vertex of one of those acute angles pointing diagonally at the concert hall, a small café keeps a few outdoor tables and hosts musicians on their spare time between rehearsals or concerts. I rarely stop at such place for I find it voyeuristic. What is the point in watching a cello player dragging his instrument followed by a long tail of disillusioned notes? Or a soprano asking for an apple martini on a high-pitched voice, the very notes she missed in her last aria? But I fight back my preconceptions and sit at a table where I am exposed to everything and everything is exposed to me. Unrecognizable as I am, people care not for my eavesdropping and carry on with their conversations. What I hear is the music of angst, of fear and jealousy, of hope—but very tame in that case. At the concert hall these musicians pour out their emotions. But in the intimacy of this outdoors café, where their words will be quickly dispersed by the wind, they pour out their wretchedness.

First a coffee, which I make last for a long time, the last sip becoming frigid. Many words and notes around me but no vision of Neva. Then a glass of wine, which I drink at once for fear it would turn into coffee. Then a glass of patience to neutralize my boiling desire for an encounter that is utterly improbable. But is it not improbability at the root of improvisation? Was I not wanting something to happen out of nothing? Only the raw, the new. That is what I told myself. So, I ask for another glass of wine and take my time to let time take its own.

Then it happens. Arising from the concert hall, a vision of Neva comes into view. With every step a note and with every note a harmony of the unknown. She approaches the café as if by chance, as if not looking for me. Or perhaps she has seen a vision of me and is indeed getting closer intentionally. She then stops her march and looks at her wristwatch. Has she lost her tempo? Has she confused the scale of her steps? She remains there, resting, listening for a cue, thinking in which direction to move next. Or simply, waiting for inspiration to guide her. I cannot tell for I cannot listen to the melody inside her mind.

When she retakes her march, it is in the direction of the café that she is heading. It is now inevitable—our paths will cross. With a swift and discrete gesture, I reach for the sound recorder inside the briefcase and turn it on. What sound will emerge from this encounter, I know not. Nothing about this encounter is rehearsed. So, only the virginal sounds of nature will be captured. My nature as the seeker of unknown melodies, her echoes perhaps better formed this time. Or maybe noise and confusion.

As Neva gets close enough to the café, I stand from my chair and wave at her. She catches a glimpse of my gesture and waves in return. Her reaction, the sum of her facial features as she recognizes me, appears to be one of surprise. As far as she is concerned, she has come across my path by accident. Nothing preordained, raw steps and chance only. I offer her the empty chair across from me next to which is the briefcase where this encounter is being sonically immortalized. Here she is now, right in front of me, the source of what I do not know, the conduit of fugitive melodies, a creator without constraints. I open the conversation with a lie.

—Neva, I wasn't expecting to see you here.

—Mr. Nicanor... Neither was I.

—Forget the "Mr." thing. Nicanor is fine—just plain Nicanor. But tell me, what brings you to the concert hall today?

—Nothing really… I had not planned to come this way, but here I found myself. I did practice some, played a few pieces, worked on technique, and listened to other people practicing. What about yourself? What brings you here today?

—I wasn't planning to come here either.

—So, we're not supposed to be here at all. But we are.

—How do you explain that?

—There's nothing to explain. Things sometimes happen.

—But things happen for a reason, don't they?

—Not necessarily. But even if they did, we don't clearly know what the reasons are. Do you always compose for a specific reason?

—I think I do, but I'm not completely sure.

—What are you not sure about?

—I don't exactly know. And that's the problem—I don't really know.

—Not knowing is just the beginning, like the silence before the first note of a piece.

—Do you always know the note you'll play next on the violin?

—Like yourself, I think I do. But I'm not completely sure.

—So, it is my turn to ask, what are you unsure about?

— and everything, which is to say, the totality of what there is.

I believe she is being honest. What can we be sure about? Perhaps the root of a composition or its tempo. But all of that can change in an instant. For example, Neva is in front of me right now, but she could be gone the next second. I could talk to her for a century and fail to unearth her true self. The truth is that after exchanging a few phrases with each other, I have learned nothing about her. I am in the not knowing—the first silence.

—Nicanor, will you be coming to our last rehearsal?

—Why do you ask?

—Well, you didn't seem to enjoy the previous one. You seemed distracted, even bothered.

—What gave you that impression?

—Nothing and everything.

—That's precisely the case. I thought that nothing was missing from Composition No. 33. But you seem to think otherwise. You implied that everything is missing.

—No, not everything… Just a few notes. That's all.

—Then, please tell me what those notes are.

Neva looks at me, but I sense she is trying to see beyond me. She ushers in another first silence that could only be followed by those missing notes. I wait for a while, but I hear nothing. She must be looking for the notes in faraway forests or maybe deep inside her own self. Or perhaps she is not looking for the notes, but instead, she is letting them arrange themselves, encouraging them to come forward in their raw and extemporaneous way. I am not certain what to expect from her. All I can do is finish my glass of wine and wait for an answer to my question. Yes, I facilitated this encounter, but I have no control over its outcome. I dare not say a word. Let the silence expand and swamp us both. So, I rest quietly, expectant, for what appears to be a rather long time, until Neva finally looks at me again, this time actually seeing me. Then she talks.

—The notes are the notes, like the silence is the silence. They are nothing and everything.

After saying those words, she stands from the chair and turns her back to me. The only echo of her, I manage to construe, is that of her steps as she walks away from the table.

#

I look out the window of my apartment, hoping to find the moon suspended in the purple. The moon is there, and that gives me a certain degree of comfort. I know I cannot control the moon. I cannot instruct it to show its face. However, it pulls and attracts me without wanting to do so. It does not sing, the moon, but it listens to my music and my questions. Although it has never answered, this night could be different. I ask the moon if it knows about Neva, about her violin, and the music she plays in the concert hall and in those alternative places. I also ask the moon if it knows about the stillness that Neva seems to inhabit. The moon does not respond; it just shines its light on me. I accept the light and bathe in it.

Why did Neva walk away from me? She offered me her silence as if she were offering everything—then she vanished. The silence felt like nothing to me, but she implied that nothing and everything are one and the same. Silences are only relative; a sonic presence is always there. So, what do we really hear when we hear nothing? I wonder what Neva heard when I was hearing nothing. Perhaps she was in tune with the melody inside her mind, a melody I could not hear. She clearly wanted to convey something to me, and she did. It is up to me to unravel what that was.

I sit at my studio where my new composition rests on its back, ignored, accumulating dust and age. Most of my new musical ideas have already made it into the score. Some empty spaces remain. A few passages are inconclusive and yearn for an organic and natural sound. I know the sound that is missing. I just cannot grab it because it does not emanate from within myself. It is a melody exterior to me, errant, elusive. I focus on the moonlight for possible answers. This unblemished moonlight enters through the window and creates a pearlescent pool on the floor of my studio. Maybe it wants to talk to me. I listen carefully to what the moonlight is saying. But I hear nothing. Those are light waves, not sound waves—they are essentially mute.

If nothing and everything are the same, the fact that I heard a silence does not eradicate the possibility that sound was indeed present when Neva and I were in front of each other. Maybe I am not sensitive enough to listen to the nuances of Neva's thoughts, those notes that irradiate after we cease talking. Perhaps my expectations overwhelmed my auditory sense, and I simply missed the melody of her mind. I cannot place complete trust in my capacity to listen. No, I should not trust myself.

I fetch my briefcase and pull out the sound recorder. This machine has no mind of its own, so it cannot be tricked. It registers the natural frequencies of the world and plays them back unadulterated. It is a brutish creature but loyal to the truth. I select the latest recording and begin to listen to the sonic pulse. First, I hear my voice, which I cannot recognize as mine. But I know it is mine; thus, I accept it. Then I hear Neva's voice as she calls my name. Her voice sounds exactly as I remember it, confirming the recorder is honest. As the conversation flows, I come to realize that we reveal very little about each other. There are more questions than answers. Then, I hear when Neva keenly observed my seemingly distracted behavior during rehearsals. I was not distracted. Scared perhaps, but not distracted.

Then comes the silence. It slips into our reality like a thief, slowly, carefully, but with unambiguous intent. It grows and encumbers everything, leaving no trace of our voices. What the recorder now plays back is a void, beautiful and pristine, like the sound of a feather floating in the morning air. I wait for a while, but the recorder offers nothing other than quietness. And as I prepare to accept the futility of this exercise, I hear a few simple notes tearing the silence apart. I listen carefully to the recorder's version of a reality that initially seemed mute to me. They seem shy, the notes, as they lay down the rudimentary structure of an emerging melody. I think I know these notes, and I think I know the melody they are introducing. So, I try to weave the notes together and compose the fugitive melody that only arrives when not expected. But the melody turns around; it plays outside of itself. It shows a little of its face for a moment before it mutates, transposed, and syncopated. It becomes an echo of itself. The rhythm is displaced. It shifts and hides from me. Then, it resurfaces but is altered, raw, new, and changed. For a moment, I wonder if this is a figment of my imagination. I quickly look at the sound recorder and confirm that it is playing that which it recorded when Neva and I were in the middle of what I thought was an immense silence. But it clearly was not.

What I am hearing is the melody inside her mind. It is not my melody but hers. This melody contains the backbone of the one that eludes me. Or perhaps hers is the original melody, and the one I sometimes hear is an alteration. Regardless of the direction in which these melodies have evolved, the fact is that I failed to hear the one that emerged from Neva's mind. I was deaf to it. Something inside of me rendered that moment a still one. If those are indeed the missing notes she refers to, how will I ever hear them?

Before I manage to assimilate the multiple variations of the innocent melody, a new silence has taken hold of the sound recorder. Once again, I hear nothing. I fiddle with the volume knob and bring it as high as possible. Silence, then silence again, until it gets interrupted by the beating of my heart. I turn the recorder off and tune in to the sound of my body. Nothing special, just blood rushing through veins and a heart pumping. No harmonies, no remnants of past melodies. The first silence is gone. The second silence is gone as well. However, Neva's melody remains in the bowels of the recorder.

For a moment, I consider rewinding the recorder to immerse myself again in the alchemy of Neva's interpretation. But what would I be listening for? Her intention behind the notes she played? Her manner of connecting one note with another? The way she was trying to express something to me? Even if she wanted to express something, why did she not use her words? Because music speaks more clearly? And if that were the case, what I heard when sitting in front of her was nothing, just that silence. Maybe I am incapable of listening.

Intent on finding an explanation, I turn the brutish creature back on and continue to listen until the end of the recording without rewinding. Yes, the notes are the notes, and the silence is the silence. And her steps are her steps, and her echo is nothing but an echo I cannot decipher. This is what I heard today, and it will not be repeated. So, I make sure to delete the recording of our encounter, now creating a third silence.

#

Neva transmitted something to me that now lives within me. She did so unintentionally, which makes her act more noble. I was the one searching for her. I concocted the encounter. She had no presentiment that I would be waiting for her arrival at that café. What she shared was already within herself. Those notes had not been predetermined or rehearsed. They were natural to her and somehow entirely identifiable to me, even in their reconstructed state. I wonder what is at the core of this mutual experience. Why do we savor a similar nectar?

There must be revealing elements lurking somewhere. The truth is that I know essentially nothing about her. And this time, nothing is not everything—it really is nothing. To learn more about her, I will have to observe her in a genuine environment where she is free from encumbrances. The concert hall is the wrong place, all stiff and codified. Plus, showing up there as a composer creates a barrier around me. I need to be free to observe her being free. Only then would I be able to savor her nectar.

I feel the pull and the fear at the same time toward the night. Yes, toward the night, I must go and descend once again into that alternative world of unbound music. What if I become unbound myself? What if all my learned structures come crashing to the floor? What if I hear notes that affect me like a suicide? Maybe that is the price to pay for knowing. If I search, I may find something, and that is the risk.

I come around *The Cave of the Forgotten* when daylight

is still lingering. I do not want any of the light to shine on my face, so I take cover under an awning across the street and wait anxiously for the night to settle. Gradually, the shadows arrive, bringing in tow the first few patrons who quickly descend into the bowels of the club. Then come a few people with cases strapped to their shoulders, musicians, I guess. I wait in the hopes of seeing Neva arrive, knowing very well that there is no certainty of her showing up tonight. Does she come here every night, every week, or only when the need to express herself boils over? Nothing, nothing still…

When the street empties out, I take advantage to make it over to the door of the club without being noticed. There is no live music playing yet. All I hear at the top of the stairs are the distant voices of people in febrile anticipation. With utmost discretion, I make my way into the club and look for a table as far away from the stage as possible. I will not be able to see the musicians very well, but I will hear every single note. The waiter comes around and asks me what I want. I cannot tell him what I want, but I ask for a glass of wine. He invites me to take a table closer to the stage. I thank him for the offer but explain that this table is perfect for me. He then asks me if I am waiting for somebody else. I say that I do not know who; in fact, it is that I am waiting for. He must have understood, for he does not ask further questions and immediately goes to fetch the wine.

Anticipation floats in the air. People talk to each other, drink libations, and keep an eye on the empty stage. Musicians and their instruments will soon occupy the territory of the stage. But what people seem to anticipate the most is the unexpected musical experience. They know who the musicians are, but they have no idea what these musicians will play. And the less they know, the more interested they appear. My expectations are different. I need to experience Neva unbound, loose, and expressing herself without a safety net. I need to witness her ascension.

A man then walks up to the microphone, convinces himself that it is working properly by blowing air into it, and announces that the concert is about to begin. He then introduces the musicians one by one as they take their respective places on the stage. At the piano... On Drums... On bass... On sax and clarinet... And playing a wicked violin...

She is here. She has arrived. I cannot see her from my table, and neither can she see me. And that is perfect, for what I need to focus on is the sound of her soul as it traverses her mind, her heart, her hands, the strings, the air, my ears, and eventually my mind, where I will try to decipher who she really is. All these transformations in a fraction of a second, but with repercussions that could be eternally profound. I investigate the abyss of possibilities and try to fathom its depth. I cannot see the bottom. So, I close my eyes and accept the risk.

The ensemble begins to play, and people continue to talk. The music pushes against the noise cloud inside the cave but advances little. Only a few clear notes reach my ears back where I am sitting. The rest are muffled by smoke and people's voices. When the first song comes to an end, I consider accepting the waiter's suggestion and move closer to the stage. But I refrain from the risky maneuver for such an exposure could alter the principle of my endeavor—Neva unaffected. I trust the noise cloud will dissipate as soon as people get touched by the music and an unchained melody cuts through them.

One song follows another, and each instrument begins to assert its voice while they become part of the unified matrix that typifies this ensemble. As their sound grows inside the cave, people begin to lower their voices and permit the music to pool inside themselves. Now, I can hear with clarity. Now, I can tune into Neva's violin. I listen to her every note and try to put them in context with the other notes played by the rest of the ensemble. She responds to every call, and her calls are answered as well. They talk to each other, invent, go on journeys, and drag the others with them. They begin and end, only to begin again and disguise an apparent ending. They glide, they touch the ground, and at times, it seems as if they touch the sky outside the cave.

Then comes a moment when Neva is playing by herself. The other musicians set aside their instruments and remain quiet. I cannot see her. I cannot watch the motion of her bow. But I can feel the pulse of every note. She is not playing a recognizable melody. I think she is playing herself. Every note is a memory or perhaps a desire. A constellation of sounds encapsulating her essence. An essence diaphanous enough to escape definition. I hear pure notes, but I also hear imperfect ones, those that make her human. She is not playing perfect; she is playing present. And this presence is different from the one that appears during rehearsals. Less defined but more defining. More porous but more condensed. By abandoning the restraints of the written score, she manages to soar high in the sky without burning herself when facing the sun.

The night deepens. The music deepens as well. Everything is played, but nothing resembling the melody I had expected to hear. Everything is nothing concerning that melody. But nothing is everything concerning Neva, for I have communed with her inner self. She is not who I thought she was. But who she is contains some identifiable traces of myself and some of the same notes. I know. I have heard them. However, she does not share those notes all the time. Tonight, she did not, but tonight is only tonight.

#

Králová… What could a name reveal? An imperfect history, an ascendency, a potential affiliation to a clan? Maybe she is the daughter of a Bohemian king. Neva Králová… All I know is that I know very little. But knowing is only half of the equation. There are feelings, sensations, or whatever we call that experience that changes the way we understand ourselves. I went down to the cave and felt something I had not felt before. Did that "something" force me to think about myself in a different way? Perhaps... Did that elicit more questions? Yes, it did. But I am not afraid of questions. They are an essential substrate of forward motion. So, I move forward.

Ahead of me is the last rehearsal, and further ahead is the concert itself. And once those two events have been consummated, there will be no natural link between Neva and myself. I would have to manufacture an encounter to come across her presence. I would see her only by means of artifice, like descending to the cave or hovering around the concert hall. A pathetic reality I refuse to accept. Perhaps those notes I identify as mine, which she seems to play as if they belong to her, would somehow link us together. She may be seeking shelter when playing those notes, a way to denude her inner world. And that is not far from my own scheme. Music is a beautiful refuge against the imperfections of the world. Maybe that is why she descends to the cave at nighttime and why I lend my hand to composing.

The day of the last rehearsal arrives without fanfare; it simply ushers itself into my morning reality and confirms that forward movement is indeed happening. I decide to focus only on Composition No. 33 and ignore any other notes or melodies that vie for attention. I will be present at the hall, listen to the quartet's interpretation, and offer my comments. I will not be deluded by underground currents where feelings lurk, by memories that question who we really are or where we come from. I will be solid and stable—if I can.

I arrive at the concert hall before any of the musicians. The rehearsal room assigned to us is virtually empty. There is no piano, just music stands, chairs, and stillness. I take advantage of this quiet moment to review the score of Composition No. 33 again. If I have the urge to make any changes, they would need to be introduced today. Avidly, I scan line after line in search of voids, equivocal harmonies, vagabond notes, and anything that could fragment the composition. I find nothing of the sort. If Neva manages to elicit unexpected elements that escape my composer's sensibility, then her inner world should be a co-author of the piece.

The four musicians arrive in unison at the rehearsal room. They seem surprised to find me here already, sitting alone, still mulling over the composition. They are here to rehearse, not to re-invent, and the idea of last-minute changes would certainly vex them terribly. But I have nothing to add or subtract from the score. So, to make them feel at ease, I greet them and declare that the composition contains all the musical elements I had intended and that it awaits their virtuous hands. "It is what it is, a complete composition that may accept a variety of interpretations." And with those words, I unchain them. I give them permission to express their individuality. Yes, I open the door to chance, such a frightening affair.

After they uncase their instruments, arrange the music stands, shuffle through the sheet music, tune to A=442, and take a collective deep breath, the quartet begins to play the first movement. They have departed on their own, tethered by what is printed on the page, but encouraged to nuance their performance. This time I do not look down at the floor or turn myself into a tormented ghost. I remain attentive and observe the oscillating movement of each bow, the creation of each note, and the construction of the edifice that supports the aural tissue of Composition No. 33.

And then, unannounced, expectations begin to fight against their strait jackets. While the rest of the quartet continue to play what is written on the score, Neva takes the liberty to add consonant and melodic embellishments while at other times she subtracts notes and creates rests. The backbone of my composition does not change, but its visage is mischievously altered. I only listen and respond not. I let chance take a chance on my score and accept the fact that creation is never finished.

I pay close attention to Neva. At any moment, she may go deep into her inner self. Whenever she touches those inner currents, notes will naturally flourish, and perhaps the very notes of the melody that escapes me. Absurd but just as plausible as any other instance when our sensibilities have coincided. She has played those notes before without knowing they have meaning to me. Or perhaps those notes have a similar meaning to her, which will explain why they arrange themselves in a particular order, molding an identical melody. I wonder if she is aware of that melody infiltrating her improvisations. I wonder what is at the root of those notes.

The more I listen, the more I marvel at the subtle alterations that Neva imparts to my composition. She uses the existing structure as scaffolding for her own expression. She does not change the piece. She simply uncovers aspects I may have ignored or perhaps aspects I may have deprived myself of expressing. What I hear is my own music, but more personal, deeper, and closer to how I understand myself and my memories. Through her interpretation, I hear more of myself. But Neva does not know me, nor can she read my mind or invent a self outside of my own self that resembles mine. Somewhere, there must be a subterranean connection I cannot understand.

The rehearsal continues uninterrupted. Every movement is played twice. When they disagree about a particular passage, the quartet asks for my opinion. But I offer no opinion; I just exhort them to play the piece in the form they think it should be played. I take care not to interfere. On the contrary, I urge them to create alongside, in parallel with me. They appreciate the freedom but understand the risk. Once they go on stage, they will be alone in front of the public. They will not be able to blame the composer for imperfections. My hand will not be the one on fire. However, in the absence of a critical audience, the less pressure to perform, the more space for Neva to reveal more of myself. So, I say nothing and listen to everything.

Once they feel that no further improvement is possible, or perhaps when fatigue has taken its toll, the rehearsal comes to an end. As I had promised myself, I did not run away. Here I am, in front of my creation, now re-created in ways I had not imagined. Mario is the first to come forward to ask if their interpretation meets my expectations. I tell him that all I had expected was for the interpretation to be an honest one. He then asks me if I think they were honest to the score or to the quartet's peculiar musical instinct. I tell him the quartet was honest to both, and with those words, I turn away from him and walk toward Neva, who is busy cleaning the rosin residue from her violin. I ask her about her last name, Králová. She refers to her Bohemian father, who fell in love with a Cuban physician sent to Prague by the Castro regime in exchange for money and political influence. After she mentions Cuba, I say nothing more.

The rehearsal went as you had expected, with an occasional blunder here and there but nothing of great importance. You played well, and you know it. You released a few hidden notes and invented some of your own. You respected the score, but you also respected your intuition. And it seems to you that Nicanor was agreeable to your explorations, perhaps even welcoming your departures and arrivals. Time will pass, and the day of the concert will come, but after your experience today, you see no reason for anything to change. You will be ready, the violin will be ready, and the music will rise to the occasion.

The only equivocal element in the entire arrangement was Nicanor's reaction when you mention who your parents were. His expression changed from placid to coagulated in a fraction of a second. Then he became silent. Maybe he does not understand what happened in Prague when numerous workers sent over from Cuba, all sorts of people, masons, plumbers, electricians, doctors, and dentists… everything. Many of them were young, like your mother. And they met locals and other foreign people. Everyone brought their own melody, and those melodies intertwined with each other forming new compositions. You are the result of such alterity; your inner sound is a mestizo one.

These are all trivial concerns. Your fundamental question is, what will happen after people stop clapping? The concert will come to an end, and your next classical engagement is not in sight. The quartet will need a new piece to work on, a new source of inspiration. But your tendency to diverge from the score has enervated a few composers and brought sinister criticism. "Who do you think you are?" You have heard that a few times. In your mind, there is a simple answer: you are who you are. And that is precisely the point. You can only play the violin in the way you play the violin—with intrusions, alterations, innovations, deletions, and everything else that needs to emerge from the interaction between the written score and the white center of yours.

If no other concerts turn up, you will be free to play any music you want and go any place you wish. There is beauty in freedom. But freedom can also be daunting, it forces you to make choices. And with every choice you make, you kill one or more alternatives. The death of those alternatives frightens you the most. You would never know how they could have impacted your life. The same happens when playing the violin; you often ignore certain notes and dismantle a melody. The unheard melody then dies in its own secrecy.

There is always Prague with its Eastern European jazz tendency and its underground clubs where you could release your uncommon notes. Nobody knows you there, you were too young when it all happened. Nobody could criticize you now. There will be freedom if your memory does not pressure you to play unsavory notes. But not all memories are somber; some radiate a beautiful light and produce an enchanting melody like the memories of your mother. Yes, she remembered her youth with gaiety infused by the beautiful melodies from her days in Cuba. But there are also the saturnine memories of the failed violinist, the monster himself.

Perhaps the best is not to decide, at least intellectually. You could decide musically. Play the violin, play it with abandon. Without expectations, without preconceived arrangements. Whatever notes emerge are the correct notes. Whatever rhythm asserts itself is the correct rhythm. Let the music play itself; it comes from within yourself, and it knows you intimately.

Recumbent on the white sofa of your small living room, the violin ignores the feat it will be asked to perform. You do not know it either, although the deep currents inside your mind are already flowing with urgency. You pull the violin out of its case and bring it up to your shoulder. There, you trap it with your chin, not with force, but with intention. Your right hand grabs the bow, and the first contact between the Mongol hair and the strings takes place. Instinctively, your fingers search for classical Bohemian roots. So, Dvorak arises. You start playing the second movement of Dvorak's Violin Concerto in A minor from memory. *Adagio, adagio... ma non troppo.* The notes glide with ease, and images of childhood autumns blur your vision. For a moment, you feel safe in the comfort of the expected. But soon, the adagio begins to gather speed; it stumbles as it propels itself forward, and it turns reckless. And the phrases become syncopated, and you taste a succulence in your mouth. You do not know what you are playing, but it feels good. So, you play, and you play some more.

Sweat begins to accumulate on your forehead. You do not care. Your left fingers stretch and perform unusual acrobatics. The bow hugs the strings and lets them go over and over. The notes aggregate in the form of a cumulus cloud, and you hear thunder. Then they seem to lie on their backs and whisper to you. So, you play, and you play some more until the moment your right hand stops bowing. The violin becomes immediately mute. The music quickly dissipates in the air, leaving no trace of itself. All those notes are now gone. What gave birth to those notes? They came from inside yourself, yes, but what do they reveal?

Prague is accessible. A direct flight will take you there in a couple of hours. The difficult part is to face a past that is not entirely clear. What if the memories suffocate you? What a paralyzing experience that would be. What about that monster? But what if the memories ignore you and leave you feeling abandoned? You have not considered that possibility, but it does exist. No, you do not have to decide. No, you do not have to move. You do not have to play a single note. You could simply die a little until the day of the concert. However, death is not an option, even if it is a partial one.

Enough, you will bring yourself and your violin to Prague. Three days and two nights is all you must open your mind. Sufficient time for your memories to inflict carnage or generate miracles. Just as the Vltava River parts the city in two, your memories are divided between the sweetness of maternal hands that did not hold you enough and the molesting hold of a paternal embrace. Nothing and everything...

You arrange the details of your flight making sure to return with adequate resting time before the concert. After some consideration, you secure a hotel close to the castle for the sense of security that imparts. Then you spend a long time searching for jazz clubs in Prague. Some are underground, and those interest you the most since you feel comfortable when descending into the bowels of the earth to unleash the notes that in turn emerge from your own bowels. And most likely, if the other musicians at the club allow you to play, you will be forgotten by the time dawn arrives.

#

Nobody knows where you are. Except for scheduled rehearsals or when there is a concert, your presence is not required anywhere. On most days, your steps are unaccounted for. You respond to yourself and to your violin—to nobody else. That is a comfortable kind of freedom carefully constructed over time. Call it solitude, but not loneliness. So, you arrive in Prague alone, with baggage and violin in tow and a mind full of memories and musical notes.

Some buildings wear a dark skin as if winter had kissed them for too long. Others are brighter, blatantly displaying their modernist façade. There are people everywhere, a legion of them. But they do not matter to you like you do not matter to them. At the front desk of the hotel the clerk asks if you will be playing a concert in town. You tell him that you will be playing but do not know what or where. He does not ask further questions and shows you to your room. You appreciate his discreet demeanor and quickly close the door behind you. Once you settle down and the sense of arrival installs itself, you pay attention to the sounds of the city. Not much can be heard inside the room, so you open the only window there is and invite the urban sounds to visit.

A cacophony, a disarray, enters with no characteristics distinguishing this from any other city. Although it is too soon to be disappointed, you had expected a swift overture into the world of your past. You listen for a while longer, but all you hear is noise; music seems absent from the street below. Chagrined, you close the window and lie on the bed to rest and forget. To remember, you first need to forget. So, you try to void your mind. And in so doing, a few loose notes pierce your awareness. They are pure and simple, but you cannot recognize them. Those could be autochthonous Bohemian notes or chimers from a Caribbean breeze. You rush to open the window with the hope of letting the notes in. But the notes do not wait for you. They become quiet and quickly evanesce.

Nighttime will fall. Until then, you will try to eradicate all ideas and concepts you have previously formulated regarding your musical past. The conservatory does not count, you were old enough then. It is the early part of your life that matters, those years when the absorption of music happened naturally. It is likely that music and words entered your mind at the same time. Without wanting to, you learned how to talk. You heard words and repeated them. And without wanting to learn how to sing, you did learn how to sing. You heard your mother's songs and repeated them as well. Both language and music are rooted deep inside the early phases of your brain development. Your words and your songs made you the person you are now. They have always been within you.

Considering that the violin is only an instrument that could not express itself without your agency, you set it aside and focus on musical memories from your infancy.

There, there, images of your mother flash by so rapidly that you have a hard time making up the details of her face, the color of her hair. It appears that she's singing, but you don't hear her voice. Then, there's a void that purple begins to fill gradually. And the more intense the color purple becomes, the more it sounds like a G flat, then a G sharp. It then loses its intensity, and it all becomes white, warm, and soothing: your center, the white center of yours.

This is where you would like to rest, rolled inside your cocoon, breathing the rarified air of innocence. Whatever emerges from this place is pure and unique. If memories emerge, then they are true. If sounds emerge, then that is the music of your very own self. However, your time in this space is shortened by the intrusion of urban sounds that somehow insist on imposing themselves. It is only natural you must accept the reality of the moment, but nonetheless, you hasten to close the window. There will be other times to be intimate with the inherent music of the town.

The names of the various jazz clubs you found mean nothing to you. Likewise, the names of the listed ensembles do not reveal the style of music they will be playing. Listing of a quartet only guarantees that four musicians will be playing tonight, but not exactly what music they will concoct. It is better to ascertain if the clubs are located underground in a cave-like environment. That matters more than anything else. So, you return to the front desk of the hotel with the list of jazz clubs in hand. You ask the clerk if any of those places is indeed an underground club. He looks at you for a second, and you sense he is trying to figure you out as if you were hiding something. Discreet once more, he places a checkmark next to two of the names and says nothing else. You then ask if the clubs are far from the hotel. He says that they are relatively close, that the problem is not getting to them but making it back, and that people sometimes lose their way. You tell him that you understand people may get confused and that perhaps that is not horrible. He does not respond to your comments.

Back in your room you look at the two names and try to imagine what sort of places they could be. The first one is called *Club Ungelt*, and the second one *AghaRTA*. The names do not reveal much. It is impossible to tell what will unfold at any of those venues. So, you pronounce the two names out loud and listen to their sonority. Both vibrate in a certain guttural way, probably Bohemian characteristics. But, somehow, *AghaRTA* seems to open itself more easily. It contains three A's and a clear symmetry. For certain, there is music at the origin of that name. That suffices for you right now.

Nighttime then falls as expected. You are full of anticipation without knowing exactly what it is you expect so ardently. But your body trembles, and your mind is eager. You will take to the streets in search of *AghaRTA,* and your violin will accompany you. That is all you know for certain; the rest is a mystery and will evolve on its own. On your way out of the hotel, you stop at the front desk once more. The clerk looks at you sideways. The smirk on his face does not bother you; he clearly battles his own demons. So, you decide to leave him in peace and refrain from asking for directions to the club. Without a map or directions, you step out on the street. You know the club is in the center of the old town. However, every building around you is old, and nothing looks precisely like a center. So, you start walking in the same direction as the crowd of tourists. After a few blocks, you arrive at a bridge lined with statues, beggars, trinket sellers, and street musicians. Those musicians will surely talk to you. You spot a guitar player who seems inspired next to his dog companion, who seems tired. Even though people from a semicircle in front of him clap with enthusiasm, his hat has barely a few coins in it. This is not the way to make a living. At the end of a song, you drop a bill in his hat and approach him. You ask him if he knows *AghaRTA*. In a familiar accent, he says he does not know that song. The jazz club, you clarify. He thinks for a second and then tells you to keep walking straight and to follow everyone to a big plaza, then to make a right turn, that somewhere in that area people go down to a cellar to hear jazz or what have you. He then asks you why you would want to bury yourself in the ground when music is available out here in the open. True, but he does not know you are traveling deep into yourself.

The crowd, the flow of disparate souls, leads the way. You do not feel like one of them, but to an onlooker you are not different. This moment you are just a small particle within a large mass in search of experiences. Every particle in the mass wants something different, but wanting is the fuel that propels the mass forward. That energy brings you to the large plaza the guitar player mentioned. To avoid diluting yourself any further, you step out of the flow and turn right as instructed. Now you feel more independent, in full control of your steps. A quick appraisal of the location reveals three streets radiating away from the plaza. They look similar, paved sidewalks, old buildings, hanging memories, but only one of them harbors the club. The search begins. You first choose the street in the middle to abort any unwanted imbalance. With every step your excitement grows a little, and gradually you start to hear loose notes. They may come from inside or outside your mind. That is not clear now. Walking and looking, walking and listening, but no sign of the venue turns up. The notes also fail to assemble themself into melodies. Nothing seems to coalesce; this is not the musical line you want to follow. So, you turn around and trace your steps back to the plaza where the crowd continues to boil.

Now you take the street on the left; that is the side of the heart. As you advance with care, the street begins to narrow down gradually to the point where opposing buildings nearly touch each other, leaving only a meager alley between them. This must be the way to the heart of the old town. You listen for music, but all you hear are your steps resonating inside the alley. The sound of your steps swells, and a pulse takes shape, a human pulse. The power of that pulse pushes you deeper and deeper into the alley. And soon you come to stand under a luminous sign that reads *AghaRTA*. This is where you descend.

#

Deep… Deep… Underground… Under the ground.

In a vast room, large enough to invalidate any sense of claustrophobia, the stage waits for the musicians to take their places. You look around, and you marvel at the sonic possibilities. The music must ascend easily to the vaulted ceiling. But having no way out, the music will need to descend, reverberating, moaning. The echo will then merge with what is being played on the stage, making the sound fatter. This is how music nourishes itself, it feeds from its own echo. The walls are covered with new and old photographs of various musicians. You recognize the notorious ones; the others must be local heroes. People have taken pictures of you, but nobody ever puts them on any wall. You would not want to be framed anyway. The stage lights are a little too bright at this moment, but that does not bother you because nobody knows who you are. Regardless, shadows will soon arrive and bathe the space in sweet anonymity.

Although you sit quietly at a table not far from the stage, the violin case speaks for you. It tells everyone that you are a musician. And since you are at a place like *AghaRTA*, you must be a jazz player. Not a mistaken assumption but an incomplete one. Just as incomplete as Nicanor's assumption that you are only a classical musician if that is what he thinks. The truth is that you have no obligation to categorize the music that comes from within you. Why draw a line in the sand if the wind will soon erase it?

A steady stream of people enters the club. All sorts of people, loners like yourself, couples, and groups stream in. They begin to occupy all available tables. An old man with a catastrophic beard asks if the seat next to you, where the violin case is resting, is taken. You say that your violin is sitting there. He says that your violin is not a person. It may not be a person, but it has feelings. You do not tell him that;

instead, you stand up and let him have the table all to himself. You need to be on your toes tonight, sitting will keep you from soaring.

The musicians finally take the stage. A pianist, a saxophone player, and a drummer. All men, as usual. There are not many female soloists in the jazz world, and you have paid your price for such an honor. People make lewd propositions rather openly. They think that if you play loosely, you must be a loose woman. There are pigs at classical venues too, but they follow the rules. They make their propositions from the heights of their power structure. However, you are not here to fix the planet. You came here in search of musical vestiges.

The idea of having a drink crosses your mind. One drink and one drink only, anything beyond that could derail your purpose. Before the concert begins, you make it over to the bar with the violin case and stand your ground. You ask for a glass of champagne and settle the bill at once. With one hand on the violin case and the other holding the glass of champagne, you feel as if you are in the middle of two worlds. One world grows from the stillness of your white center and gradually bubbles up in the form of notes, harmonies, and improvisational feats. The other begins when you drink stars, but those sparkling bubbles could fizzle you down if you are not careful. Always a duality in nature, as in your memories, as in your conception of yourself, as in your music.

The pianist begins to play a few chords. He is quickly

joined by the drum player while the saxophone remains quiet for the moment. As you had anticipated, the sound travels through the cavernous room, reverberating with a deep elegance. All the notes are heard, the harmonics are preserved, nothing is wasted. The saxophone then joins in and occupies the sonic space between the piano and the drums. They know each other very well, you can tell. They must have a history together. The music seems to be original, not a standard, probably something they composed on a Sunday afternoon over a few mugs of Pilsner. Their rhythm has a metamorphosed sway, different from what you normally hear at *The Cave of the Forgotten*. This cave has its own peculiar sound, one that seduces you.

One song follows another, and the more unchained they become, the more syncopation enters their arrangements. This is when you hear a distant call, not of Dvorak, but of a different sort, ancient and native. Not only do you hear this call, but you feel it in your body, and you want to respond to it. Yes, you can respond; that is precisely what you do when you play by yourself and improvise in full liberty. So, you decide to remain open and attentive because something in their music is resonating with you.

When the band takes a break, the three musicians come to the bar to satiate their need of alcohol and appreciation. Everybody greets them and everybody wants to talk to them. You move to the side to make room for the exchanges to happen. In so doing, you place in evidence not only your empty glass of champagne but your violin case as well.

Without wanting, you are the one calling for attention.

The pianist takes notice, disengages from a conversation that must be torturous, and comes to stand next to you. He asks if you would like another glass of champagne. Yes, you would like another glass, but you are not going to have one. So, you simply tell him that you cannot drink more champagne because you need to concentrate. He laughs and says that there is no need to concentrate on their music, that you should let the music touch you—a strange proposition, so you laugh to release your tension. Then you tell him that you are concentrating on what you will be playing soon. He looks at the violin case and nods, then asks when and where will you be playing. This is the moment when you need to be brave. You came to Prague with a purpose that will only be realized if you have enough courage. So, you look at him straight and calmly say that you will be playing with his trio in the next set. He laughs again but louder this time. Then he asks for your name. When you say Králová... Neva Králová, his expression changes and he becomes rather serious. He does not know who you are. Yes, you have a Bohemian name, but you do not belong in this city, and he must sense that. Curious now, he asks you what it is that you will be playing. You tell him that you will be playing nothing and everything, that the music will find its own way. He smiles, nods a few times, and walks back to the stage in silence.

Alone on the stage, the pianist plays to himself. You want to listen to his playing, but the loud chatter of people and the clinking of glasses mutes the sound of the piano. He seems absorbed, talking to himself by means of the music, nodding some more, living a private moment probably elicited by his brief encounter with you. Unfortunately, whatever he is playing is getting lost. You see him clearly from where you stand, and so does he for he lifts his head from time to time and gazes in your direction. After a while he stops playing and signals to his band mates to return to the stage. Those two disentangle from their conversations and join the pianist. They talk to each other briefly, look in your direction, and take their proper places on the stage. The pianist then starts playing a soft intro, the kind of music that, as he proposed, would like to touch you. People in the room return to their seats and become quiet, the music touching them, you assume. Once the ambience is set and everyone's attention is focused on the pianist, he stops playing, gets up from his bench, and announces that Ms. Králová, who recently arrived in Prague from somewhere, will join in with her violin to play nothing and everything.

You just heard what he said. He is giving you permission to express yourself. This is what you had expected—there is no room for hesitation now. So, with all the confidence in the world, you drag your violin case over to the stage. After greeting the musicians, you pull the violin out and stand facing the audience. Time then stops its march and waits for your gesture. You are about to embark in the mastery of time. What is music if not domesticated time, reproducible time, shaped time? You then begin to unleash the notes that are needed at this very moment. The piano follows your melodic line at a safe distance and the saxophone follows the piano in turn. All the while the drummer fills the background with a creative groove that glues together all other sounds. You have no idea what it is that you are playing. It could be nothing, but it could be everything at the same time. What matters is to allow for the music to emerge and find its own way, so it can bounce against the ceiling and the walls of this underground space and disquiet your dormant memories. Let your own music touch you deep, deeper.

All the notes, the note. All the melodies, the melody. You follow your instinct, and the violin follows your command. The other musicians follow your lead. The music fills the room, and it gets under your skin. What begins as a customary chord progression breaks apart into a syncopated rhythm calling you. It wants to be heard, to reveal itself to you and to the audience that seems mesmerized by the unorthodox playing, by the raw nature of the violin sound. Whose music this is, you do not know, but it feels natural, even ancestral. The drummer understands your yearning and launches himself into a clave rhythmic pattern trying to install a temporal control on the music. He tames the beast for a moment, but you set it loose again. This time the violin sound ascends in a voluptuous cadence echoing *La Habanera*. It allures, it seduces, until it disintegrates into a slower, creolized, syncopated rhythm that emboldens the piano and the saxophone to try to touch you with their notes. You allow them. The notes caress each other and whisper among themselves. They ask, "where do you come from?" They respond, "just listen and remember." You listen to all the notes and explore your memories. Images flash by, and you hear their sound. The violin gives those sounds a form and the drummer a rhythm. But what are you remembering? Is this the same music your mother sang to you? You want to ask her, but she is dead now. So, you continue playing until all the notes are released and memories run dry. Exhausted, then, you quiet down your violin.

There is origin, but there is also influence. Nature and nurture they call it. I could have been born in Vienna, but that would not have made me a Viennese composer. The blows of life and the close contact with various people are what make us who we are. Barcelona adopted me and fed me its culture and a good dose of Catalonian pride, not Spanish pride. For the world outside my consciousness, I am a composer born in Barcelona. The press release for the concert asserts such a lie; I am presented as Nicanor from Barcelona. Little matters to anyone that the truth is different. Regardless, the truth has lost its luster in the later days.

Neva did mention Cuba. I wonder if she did so on purpose. She is a sensitive musician capable of unearthing missing notes. What else can she unearth? What does she know about me? Very little, probably, but intuitively she may know everything. Or perhaps it is my fear of being exposed that creates doubts and unlikely constructs. However, there is nothing to fear, which does not mean I fear nothing. At least, what I know does not frighten me. Pertaining to what I do not know, that remains a mystery that may or may not scare me once revealed. Of course, it is entirely possible that there is nothing hidden anywhere, that everything is and has always been out in the open.

I return to my unfinished composition, hoping to leave fears and uncertainties behind. The first movement is almost complete. Although imperfect, I feel I can move ahead and tackle the rest of the piece. This time I must be completely unbiased. I should not exclude any melody emerging from any source, whether they arise from my conscious or unconscious self. Better to let the notes flow freely and arrange them once they have settled in my mind. I could also experiment with not writing anything down for a while. I could wait for the melodies to attain their own shapes. Once they are comfortable with their harmonic structures, I should audition them. They shall present themselves and tell me their stories. They may even tell me their origins. Or perhaps they will only sing their song and leave it up to me to imagine who they are, where they come from, and what haunts them.

I sit at the piano and keep my hands suspended over the keys. I then listen to the sound of the clock ticking, the sound of the wind coming through the window, and the pulsating sound of my heart. All natural sounds respect their own rhythms. Although they anchor me to what is real, these are not the notes I need at this moment. I listen some more. Three, five, ten minutes... Nothing, only the sounds of the world. But I am aware that the present world is not where I need to be. If the notes are supposed to flow with ease, I would clearly need a change of paradigm. So, I stand, close the piano, and engage my mind in the act of remembering.

A vast lunar territory, arid, dispossessed of memories—I search for signs of past experiences, for the sounds of my youth. What I hear is a sidereal void punctuated by occasional static pulses. There are no voices, nor are there melodic innuendos. I imagine time as a flowing river and swim to its source. I arrive wet as a fish and suffocated. There I listen for autochthonous sounds, but silence comes to greet me. Where have my memories gone? Why have they abandoned me? Maybe the conscious act of remembering manages to dampen the music of our past. Perhaps I should blossom as a night flower and wait for the morning dew to whisper to me. Let me not search; on the contrary, let me be found.

It then rises, a rhythm as nubile as any unbridled desire. It flirts with my senses. It lets itself be heard for a few measures before it absconds. Soon enough it resurges again, this time with more flesh to boast. What I hear is a pulse that wants to carve through me. It does not ask permission; it simply decides to make its way deep into the depository of my lost memories. The beat of the rhythm pools within myself and takes temporary residence. I abandon all preconceived ideas and allow for this rhythm to talk to me, to shine a light on the memories I no longer recognize. The rhythm then floats up to my consciousness as a simple *güajira* where the notes arrange themselves in triplets. I know this rhythm but never knew how I came to know it. It seems to be inscribed in my neural tissue from birth. So, I try to approach the rhythm, to pet it softly. To my surprise, it lets itself be touched, caressed, and that gives me enormous pleasure. I decide this will serve as the structure for the second movement of this unfinished composition. I did not look for it, the rhythm found me on its own.

But a rhythm is only a scaffolding, a point of departure. I need to write the appropriate notes on the staves and flesh out a melody telling the story I fail to remember. Or perhaps there is nothing to remember because I may not have ever known what originated this musical territory. How could I write a melody, not of the forgotten, but of the unknown? By being open. Yes, I must then be open to all currents and allow for all sensations to influence me. Somehow, by encouraging all this sensorial material to flow through me, in conjunction with so many wounded memories, the notes will manifest, and a melody will take form. Anything could then happen, ecstasy—and hell.

I listen some more, open all viable channels, render myself fertile to the seeds of any rhythm or melody. However, after the first *güajira* rhythm plays itself out, nothing else comes to greet me. I am content to have heard that rhythm, but I want more. Wanting, however, guarantees nothing, and nothing is precisely what I hear at this point. The notes hide from me, the melodies do not take form, music refuses to show its face. Despite these obstacles, I will not despair. I will not close myself to the burning magma of my inner world.

What now comes to find me are not sounds, but images of past times I cannot recall ever seeing.

There I see myself, walking among the tobacco fields where a classical sculpture of a resting lion breaks the monotony of row after row of green leaves. There I am, up in the sky, watching the white paths of delicate clouds where angels frolic. Then I see myself in the middle of the night watching the bloodied hooves of a chimera inside my bathtub. I watch myself as I am in the act of watching and wondering.

These are memories I cannot recognize. They are vivid, and they are noiseless. If any rhythm emerged from these images, it would certainly be a syncopated one, and it would undoubtedly oppose and push against the form.

I let my hands fall on the piano keys. A strident sound fills the room, an explosion sending notes running for cover, pure chaos and disorder. I strike the piano keys again without any intention. An uncomfortable dissonance confirms that I am not aligned with any musical current. Before I hit the keys again, I stop myself in mid-air and look at my fingers. They are confused, they are behaving as deranged mechanical objects without a consonant purpose. Let me bring this aberration to an end, let me rest my hands on my lap and focus my attention on the images that parade in front of my mind's eye.

I see myself as a young boy in the middle of a gathering of old people. They all pay attention to me as I recite from memory the verses of a poem I cannot recognize. The words that escape from my mouth have no meaning to me, but they produce a rhythm that resonates with some of my feeble memories.

I hone on that rhythm, I let it fill me. Then I raise my hands and land them softly on the piano keys: no force, no agency, no urgency. My fingers trace the image of my young self articulating the words of the poem, they play the appropriate notes and reproduce the rhythm of my young voice. I let myself go and marvel at the peace this rhythm induces on me. I just play my visual memories as if they were the score of my virtually forgotten youth. There is joy and legitimacy in my playing, and there is also the fear that I will never write this music because the moment my memories begin to fade, when I cannot see my young self any longer, the rhythm stops, and stillness re-emerges.

I bring my hands together and close my eyes. The silence takes hold of the space outside and inside my skull. I do not see, nor do I hear anything. As for the memories, they have vanished entirely. Out of this void and nothingness, everything will emerge like a star from a sidereal vacuum, our earth from elemental magma, or a symphony from virtual quietude. I must draw inspiration from the earliest sounds, from the first images, from the faintest memories. That is the origin.

#

Everyone who could have known the entire story has either died or lost his or her memory. There is no repository for my past. The narrative of my origin, if there is one, is not available to me. There are no words to articulate the events that occurred during the passage of that period. I can reconstruct a history to suit my needs, but a fictional account that would be. In essence, what I know about my past is limited to that which I can remember. And that handful of memories are fluid and erratic, minimal, and often surreal. Music, on the other hand, does not lie or mislead. It floods our mind where it remains until summoned. Nobody needs to remember it; no account needs to be established. It lies dormant in a precious room within our brain. Then, when the appropriate alignment of memories occurs, music forces its way to the forefront of our consciousness and becomes manifest. It does not explain itself; it simply saturates our sonic perception and we hear it as the soundtrack of our past.

What I hear, then, is an honest representation of my early childhood. I cannot tell what the color of the sky was, nor who the people around me were. I cannot tell if I was happy or sad. All that becomes apparent is a rhythm. A rhythm that feels natural to me but that exists outside of the classical canon. A rhythm autochthonous to Cuba where my roots are supposed to be hugging the ground. But whose ground? Am I supposed to draw sustenance from a land I no longer feel under my feet? Am I indebted to the music I heard in the womb? Perhaps I am, the rhythm seems to imply so. Or at least, the rhythm does not seem to care, it simply charges the air with its careless cadence. I am the one responding in neural ways. So, then, let me stop…

If I could, I would love to encounter Neva and hear what she has to say about the missing notes. She has a special response to Composition No. 33, that is clear. She seems to identify aspects of that composition that escape me, even if

I wrote it myself, alone or in the company of mischievous memories that hide from me. She may be responding to that composition from her own bank of naughty memories. We may both be sourcing a past that is not evident to neither of us. Of course, that is only a speculation on my part, a dangerous way to find answers.

I should talk to Mario. With only a few days left before the concert, my call will certainly alarm him. He may think I will criticize his playing or ask him to change his performance. He may not even answer my call to avoid any conflict. I should not blame him for avoiding me completely. So, I will call him nonetheless. Anyway, when I search my list of contacts, Mario's telephone number is nowhere to be found. I do not recall ever calling him, so that makes sense. What does not make sense is to find Neva's telephone number listed among my contacts. I have never called her; I do not even know who she really is. Her number is there by mistake or by miracle. I cannot tell.

I consider the number for a while. It suggests a link where there is no link. It implies a closeness that does not exist. Despite that, my first instinct is to call her. But first instincts are often deadly and lead us astray. How could I approach her directly if I have never established a personal relationship with her? There is no logical reason for calling her other than my conjectural concerns about a childhood melody that she might recognize. And why would that be relevant at this point when what really matters is the upcoming concert? Yes, that is the rational mindset—follow the expected path. But if I am to be found, I must then fall off the five lines and four spaces.

I call the number. The ringing tone has its own rhythm, persistent, unflaggingly precise. It may not be the same sound that Neva hears, her phone may render the sound differently, but it must be just as tireless. I wait for her to answer. I wait. I wait some more. But there is no response to my call. I look at the name linked to the number once more. Yes, Neva is the correct name even if I cannot explain how that name found its place in my list of contacts. I call the number once more and hold my breath. This time a woman's voice answers the call. It does not say much, just a simple "Hello." The timber of the voice is familiar to me, but I cannot ascertain if it belongs to Neva. I feel the impetus to start talking and tell this woman that I am Nicanor, that I want to talk to Neva, that there is a melody she might recognize that I cannot capture but that I need desperately, that perhaps we have roots in common, and lastly, I am not a creep harassing people on the phone. But I reign in my impetus and remain quiet; I say nothing—I simply listen. And the listening yields nothing for beyond that first "Hello," a noiselessness follows.

Maybe silence is the answer. Silence, a negation or a possibility? For music to occur, it must emerge out of silence. Therein the procreative capacity of silence. Perhaps my mistake is to search for a fugitive melody within the realm of other melodies, as opposed to a search within the realm of silence itself. If Neva answered that phone call and provided me with a sonic void after a simple greeting, she must have understood what I need at this point. But how could she know it was me calling? Even more complicated, how could she know what I am searching for? She could not have known any of this unless she is also in the process of searching.

I break away from my rumination and push aside my composition. What I need at this moment are not those ephemeral notes but understanding. I can always return to my composition at a later point. It will not disappear, it will wait for me, recumbent on its back, fantasizing about that old rhythm of my youth. So, I leave my apartment in haste and head for the concert hall where, if I am lucky, I will find Mario rehearsing for the upcoming performance. Even though he is an abstruse creature, which Mario clearly is, he may be inclined to share with me some information about Neva. However, I would need to proceed with care for he may interpret my interest in Neva as a predatory move. I am not a predator, far from that, but Mario does not know that.

My path to the concert hall takes me through streets I rarely take. I am aware of my circumambulation but accept it as a soothing maneuver before confronting an uneasy situation. Once I arrive, I glide quietly from one rehearsal room to another in search of Mario's sound. I hear all sorts of instruments but not a single cello. I do hear violins rehearsing Bach, even Sibelius. Cellos, however, are nowhere to be heard. Maybe his neighbors are rather tolerant and allow him to rehearse in his apartment. Or perhaps he feels that he knows Composition No. 33 well enough and needs no further practice. Regardless of the explanation, Mario is not here and that irritates me. Yes, I am irritated because I feel like a predator and that is not what I am.

Disappointed, I leave the concert hall before anyone recognizes me. People like to inquire about upcoming concerts, never about past ones. And I am not in the mood for talking about my own music when aspects of it remain mysterious to me. I move fast, but not fast enough to miss Mario's silhouette sitting at the café in that perilous angled street where I once met with Neva. I stop on my tracks and regard him from the distance. It is him, Mario, and he is alone. Not knowing what the outcome of this exchange will be, I direct my steps toward him. This time I am the one approaching from afar, gradually, my heart thumping, like the predator I am not supposed to be.

When I come in full view, Mario waves at me with that pure and ancient gesture of recognition. He seems surprised to see me, but not necessarily content. As soon as I reach his table, he invites me to take a seat. I accept his offer and act as if I was not expecting to see him around here, as if I had not left my apartment with the clear intention of finding him. Now that I am in front of him, I must be prudent, but at the same time, I need to extract precious information from him without causing alarm.

—Mr. Nicanor, I hadn't expected to see you around here.

— Forget the "Mr." thing. Nicanor is fine. Just

plain Nicanor.

—As you wish, Nicanor. But do tell me, how does it feel when one of your compositions is about to enter the world? What is it like for you?

—Well, how does it feel to play a new composition in front of a live audience?

—That depends on the composition. But, to begin with, there's always fear. Then there's a moment when you believe in yourself and trust that your skills will live up to the expectations of the audience and the composer. Then you must perform the piece. That's the real test because once a note is played, you cannot retrieve it, it was either the correct one, or it was not. It must be like a person walking on a tightrope, a false step could be costly.

—Do you enjoy that sensation of fear?

—I'm not sure. I run away from it, but other times I run toward it. How about yourself, Nicanor, are you afraid we won't perform your composition with grace and mastery?

—No, that's not my concern at this moment. I'm more concerned about the way you and your fellow musicians feel when playing my music. What does it mean to each of you?

—I can only speak about myself. For me, the real meaning will become clear only after the piece is performed in its entirety in front of an audience. Whatever happens before that is only conjecture.

—Yes, I understand your position. How about Neva, how do you think she feels about my composition?

—I guess you'll have to ask her directly.

—But she's not here at this moment. Do you know where I could find her?

—I believe she's in Prague. I don't know for what reason, but she hinted at that just the other day.

—Why Prague?

—That's where she's from. Or at least that's where her father is from. Her mother came from the islands.

—Does she ever play that music?

—What music?

—The music of the islands.

—I've never heard her play anything other than classical music.

—How about jazz?

—What about jazz?

—Nothing, nothing…

Nothing is precisely what I learn from Mario; only that he ignores a critical facet of Neva's life. I know about some of her secrets by chance, or perhaps by the grace of shadows, those shadows that reveal more than the light we revere so much.

#

Prague… I could lose myself there. Or perhaps I could find myself there. I could also look for Neva all over Prague and not find her. On the other hand, I could look for her and actually find her. What would I do if I happen to find her? It is also possible for me to go to Prague and not look for her at all. In any event, chance could produce a fortuitous encounter. I could come across her in a bright plaza, in a dark alley, in the bowels of a jazz club. But what are the odds of that happening? Minimal at best. However, if I decide to stay here, paralyzed, I will never know if I would have found her. The same dilemma occurs in music. The dormant score of an unplayed symphony does not exist until acted upon by musicians. Once played, we know its miracle and limitations. Thus, I must walk through the streets of Prague to hear my echo, the music I produce in the process of looking for Neva. Otherwise, nothing would be heard, and nothing would be known. It is also possible that she went to Prague in search of her own echo. If that were the case and we happen to walk through the same old streets, would we produce the same sounds, the same music? Perhaps our steps sound the same; however, the music we hear is tinted by those early memories that color our lives. Thus, each of us would hear a different interpretation. But if both versions are similar, with equal melodies and tempo, then a parallel in our early memories must be modulating those sounds.

Yes, it seems like a futile exercise: to leave for a city barely known to me in search of a fugitive melody. But I cannot restrain myself from going. I wonder what it is that I am really looking for. Is it the melody—or Neva? Are they one and the same? Or is Neva a subterfuge my mind employs in its quest for discovery? It feels like I need to unearth, to turn around the soil, to unsettle my condition as a composer of expected music. I have no clear idea where to start my search once in Prague. I have no plan. I would need to improvise my steps.

Two days, three days… I do not have that much time. Perhaps I should cancel the concert until I find all the notes that should be contained in Composition No. 33. No, wait, that is a foolish thought, all the notes are already there, they just need to be released. To find Neva is to find the notes. To find the notes is to reveal something that appears to hide from me. There is no use in thinking about it any further. I must go even if I am not sure of what is there to be found.

I will bring my simple self and my fragmented memories. I will leave behind my composer's self. The purpose is to find, uncover, and identify notes, not to arrange them as an agreeable melody. This is not the time for creating musical structures, passages, or even a simple lullaby. I am going to Prague to listen. I may find loose notes, maybe even Neva's voice—I shall see. As for tools, I bring my sound recorder, my open mind, and the hope that my memories will not distort what I am about to hear. I also bring a phone number that so far connects only to silence.

#

The Vltava River splits the town in two. I choose the side where the ground is higher and stay near the old castle.

From here I can descend to the town center and rummage for sounds. Upon my return, some notes will follow me up the hill because notes have that tendency, they ascend when turned loose. From my hotel window I can see spires, red roofs, and an exuberant mist that is certain to modulate those same notes. And from that mist a memory emerges.

There I am at a young age, walking alone through Wenceslas Square when I hear Spanish words coming out of a lively café. I recognize the cadence and the sultriness of the Cuban accent. Without hesitation I enter the café and identify the native source of those words. Two men, dressed in working clothes, nurse a couple of beers and talk to each other with unbundled enthusiasm. They seem happy, or perhaps relieved after having finished the toil of the day. I order a pilsner for myself, approach the two men, and ask them what brings them to this part of the world. Their enthusiasm deflates the very instant they hear my voice. One of them, the one with a short beard, asks me the same question: what brings me to this part of the world? What's evident is that neither of us belongs here, that we are in this old town for different reasons, and that those reasons may not be in unison. We are about the same age, a fact that places us immediately in combative mode—the curse of young males. I say I'm traveling, something they must have guessed for I'm not dressed like they are. They tell me they are here for work. We toast and that eases the tension slightly, only slightly.

The one with the beard makes an interesting remark. He says that my Cuban accent isn't pure, that I must have lived elsewhere. I tell him that I've lived in many places. This answer, however, doesn't seem to satisfy him for he still looks at me with a suspicious eye. His partner, on the other hand, pays little attention to me or to our conversation and seems more concerned with his beer and the young woman standing next to him with a cigarette in her hand. I decide to inquire further and ask the bearded one what kind of work they do. This question brightens his facial expression and opens the floodgates. He says that they are here on a mission to build, to help this country move forward and achieve the greatness it deserves, that they do the hard work some of the locals don't know how to do, and that their skills are second to none. They are proud to represent the profound goodness of the Cuban people, that the wisdom of their leader is evident and clearly manifested by setting up this initiative, this mission of universal redemption. I wonder if his fervor is genuine or beer inspired, I cannot tell. I then ask what kind of work they do. He says that they are masons, and proud of it.

The bearded one continues to look at me with some kind of disdain. I sense he's curious, but something holds back his questions. Maybe he doesn't want to know much about me, or maybe he wants to know more but fears he'll dislike me even more. He then gets the attention of his partner and tells him, commands him: "We need to figure this one out." With aplomb and gravity, he asks me how old I was when I left. I've left many places in my life, but I understand what he means. I tell him I left Cuba with my family when I was six years old, a guess, for I'm not sure how everything happened. His demean-

or changes abruptly, the acute angles of his face soften, his eyes now closed in what appears to be a deep sense of relief. He leans toward me and gives me a strong hug. I feel his beard against the left side of my face as he whispers in my ear: "Then, it wasn't your fault."

We toast again. This time the two of them are brimming with joviality. They start talking about what it is like to be a guest worker, about their families in Cuba who understand the need for their international mission, about the sense of fraternity among all foreign workers, and especially about the satisfaction derived from their labor. We toast to our fortuitous encounter, proof that destiny is ultimately wise and well-meaning. We carry on conversing and drinking until the late afternoon, when we part ways and promise to meet again soon somewhere in the old town. I watch them as they walk down the street; they seem genuinely happy. What surprises me, however, is that at no point in our alcohol-fueled conversation had they asked another question about my current situation. It appears that my life after age six is of no consequence to them, a gangrenous part of me that needs extirpation.

Maybe that is exactly how that encounter took place. Or perhaps my memory interprets the encounter in such a way. Regardless of the accuracy, I have not encountered that memory in a long time. It emerges now because of the misty air of Prague, or perhaps because of the divisive power of the Vltava, which cuts through the unity of land and mind, or because the hope of finding an old melody weakens my resistance. There is a membrane in our minds sealing away old, conflicted memories. When that membrane becomes porous, we are about to see ourselves in a different light—I sense the danger.

#

I wait for daylight to exhaust itself before stepping out of the hotel. Not because I am afraid of exposure or recognition. After all, nobody in this town knows who I am. I do not know who I am myself. But that is a different problem. The mist has not lifted; it now engulfs the lampposts giving their light a yellow patina that digs into my soul in search of remnants of sadness. I offer none. On the contrary, I welcome the subdued tonality, for it calms my angst. Even though I am here on my own account and initiative, I am aware that realities and memories may twist and turn my self-perception. So, I proceed with caution.

My first instinct is to meander through the old town and allow random events to shape my experience. But upon further consideration, I come to realize the inherent perils in that exercise. Memories may assail my vulnerable mind and derail my purpose. I may be burdened with the weight of a past I may not be prepared to understand. Better to guide my steps with intention, even if such an attempt proves futile since I know very little about this town. Regardless of my ignorance, I begin my descent into streets and alleys in full awareness.

My passage is rather fluid until I arrive at the banks of

106

the river. It does part the land in two. I wonder if people are the same on both sides of the river or if there are meaningful differences between them. After all, the castle does not straddle the river, so it must significantly influence its surroundings. I am staying on the side where the castle is located, where my composer's mind wants to exert control. But then there is the other side, the one I know little about, which frightens me. That is the side that absconds melodies and where bewildering memories may lurk.

The bridge welcomes me with its statues and street musicians and shows me the way to the other side. Once I cross it, I turn around and regard the hill from where I just descended. It rests there, placidly, bathed in that minty mist which blurs sharp edges and difficult thoughts. I will return there after exploring and exposing myself. So, I continue my jagged march through the heart of this town that has seen horrible conflicts throughout history. Mine, in comparison, is a rather modest conflict—how to accept that certain notes and melodies elude my capture. On the surface it appears to be a banal preoccupation. The problem is that a woman I barely know seems to master those same notes and melodies. And, somehow, that woman senses my struggle and frustration for she offers those notes to me, perhaps unconsciously, and then takes them away. Then there is the question of the past. A rather uneasy question that is.

My steps bring me in front of a place called *AghaRTA*. The sign at the door says that "Everybody goes to *AghaR-*

TA." I do not know who everybody is nor why would they want to come to this place. My body, it seems, must be part of that "everybody," for I came to this place without knowing that I wanted to come here. It appears to be a jazz club since the word "jazz" is written all over the sign. I accept this reality and pause to explore my memories. Is it possible that I have just retraced a path that belongs to an instance in my past? Or perhaps not; simply being part of "everybody" suffices to bring me here. I cannot tell, and it may not matter.

The natural order of things would be for me to enter the club in search of musical memories. But jazz as a musical expression forms no part of my past—at least, no part of my musical education. I was formed within the classical, often neurotic, conservatory system. We never improvised, that was the labor of the devil. We rendered homage to the established canon, the music of the royal, ecclesiastical, or intellectual powers. We were trained to interpret, not to invent. And that is what I have been doing all these years as a composer, constructing layer upon layer of expected melodies aligning with someone else's past. So, what would I be looking for inside this jazz club? A loose melody, a buried memory, a woman who improvises? Perhaps all of that, or perhaps nothing at all, which, according to Neva, could very well be everything. I trespass the door.

Down, down, down into the bowels of this old town. The arched ceiling forms a cavernous space that must have hidden something other than music in the past. Lives could get trapped here, dreams as well. In the absence of natural light, the electrical fixtures accentuate the amber color of the stone walls. Those stones equally reflect sound and probably create a warm resonance which may be the reason for placing the jazz club in this hole. Or perhaps the music needed to be hidden, kept away from the defenders of the canon.

The stage is empty, the tiny tables are half-empty, and nobody is at the bar. There is no sense of expectation. If music is to happen here, it will be later or perhaps on a different day. But none of that really matters. What truly matters is that I have accepted the invitation presented to me by the vagaries of chance, and I am ready to listen to what the underground of this town has to offer. So, I occupy a table and invite myself into the nothingness of the moment. And as soon as I settle down,

…the memory of a young woman with pale blue eyes comes into view at a nearby table. She shares the table with her mother and her stepfather, who was the perpetrator of the abuse, as I later learned or intuited. I am not sure. The image contains music, a clarinet exuding notes, a battery holding the ground, and a sense of strangeness that could be a result of my own uneasiness in this town that still stinks of Russian influence. But these are different times now. What I see in front of me is the diaphanous film of a weak memory that emerges at will without consideration for my readiness. I close my eyes, but memories do not pass through our retinas. They are stamped directly onto the glandular matter of our brain cells. So, I stop

thinking...

The thinking does not stop, on the contrary, it accelerates and reveals that the blue-eyed girl is unwell and that if a melody could describe her situation, it would be a fado or some other distressed musical expression.

The image vanishes when a waitress interrupts my thought process to ask if I want something to drink. All at once reality enters my awareness and I find myself looking at this waitress who does not look like the blue-eyed girl. I tell her that what I need is not a drink but understanding. She looks perplexed but manages to ask what it is that I need to understand. I tell her that I need to understand nothing and everything. She laughs. Perhaps she understands. Red wine, I say to her.

As time elapses, life in the underground begins to evolve. With the arrival of the future audience or more appropriate accomplices, the base volume of the space increases, attaining the level of a basso continuo, albeit not musical at all. This is the sound of life when contained within a closed cavern, a human sound, but not necessarily beautiful. Music serves itself well from reverberation and impulse responses, but our collective human buzz needs open spaces to eviscerate itself. But the heightened human sound injects the space with a sense of expectation that was missing just a while ago. It is now evident that music is about to happen. So, I decide to wait and listen.

I know what I am waiting for. I also know that the chances of hearing Neva play her violin in this setting are minuscule. For what reason would she be scouring the undergrounds of Prague? She is clearly not looking for me like I am looking for her. That is obvious. However, she could be in search of memories, and memories are often buried. But the fact that I respond in a certain way to my uneasiness does not mean that she needs to respond in the same way. I proceed with intention. If her way of playing jazz is any indication of how she searches for the unknown, then she would improvise her approach. That means she would be loose and unencumbered rather than anxious and frustrated like that way I feel right now.

The waitress arrives with a glass of red wine, which she places on the little table. She tells me that the wine may help me gain some understanding, that she has seen patrons of this club change dramatically after two or three glasses, and that some of them have even become enlightened in conjunction with the music. I ask her how she could tell when someone became enlightened. She tells me she does not know but can see it on people's faces. I believe her. I need some enlightenment by way of music or alcohol, preferably by way of remembering, which may be ushered by one or the other of those two.

The evening advances. People keep on invading the space. The human sound escalates until the moment when a rather scraggly man walks over to the stage and introduces a hush larger than himself. The audience listens to his announcement: "Tonight, we have the pleasure of the unusual; that is, our traditional trio will be joined by a guest violinist who is certain to entice your interest in world music. What is world music? you may ask. Just listen." This is exactly how he prepares the audience for the upcoming musical experience. In my mind, he can only be referring to Neva. But what do I really know? I know nothing, but I fear much. So, I get on my feet at once, call on the waitress to settle my bill, and ascend to the street level, where the stone walls reflect the sound of my fugitive steps as I walk away.

Do

Last night left you with a sense of bewildered freedom. You played the music you felt like playing, and the trio accompanied you perfectly. The audience applauded without knowing the extemporaneous nature of the music. They probably thought you had practiced with the trio before. It was all natural; the boiling memories produced a sound that blended with musical expectations that neither the other musicians nor the audience knew were brewing within them. It could not have happened in any other way. Naturally, you want to live through that experience again. You want to descend once more into that cave to release the notes that yearn to come out. All the notes, all of them…

But the hours must parade through the daytime before nighttime can appropriately fall. Why not use those hours for something genuinely useful? Like, for example, learning more about the imprints of your mother. If you search, you may find something you do not know. Your mother inhabited this town and must have left a trace, even though she said she never belonged here. Maybe her heart did not properly belong here. However, her songs were not her heart, and those songs can reside anywhere. You just heard them last night. Maybe everything is everywhere; you just need to look and listen.

She must have had a routine: streets she traversed daily, people with whom she often spoke, places from where she looked at the river. Nobody told you what those patterns were, but they must have existed. Your mother said she did not remember. Maybe she needed to bury everything that belonged to that period. And by burying everything, she ended up with nothing. When she went back to her island, she only carried her songs with her. You were one of those songs.

First, to the river; it is likely she formed a strong relationship with that flowing body of water. Your mother was also flowing differently, but flowing nonetheless. Both bodies were here at the same time. The river continued its course within its ancient bed. Your mother eradicated herself from the course that brought her to this town for complicated reasons. She cannot be visited, your mother. But you can visit the banks of the river and watch as its waters undulate and reinvent themselves constantly.

You prepare for the long journey. You will parade along with the hours in search of unnoticed miracles, those flashes that illuminate dormant memories. You have no expectations, no guarantees, only the hope that a certain alignment of sounds, images, and chance will convey clarity of past events or—at a minimum—conjure music that touches you deeply. The violin will naturally accompany you because you already know the destiny that awaits you once nighttime falls. On your way out of the hotel, you ask the clerk if the river changes much throughout the course of the year. He says that it seems to grow in the spring and that it changes its color every day to match that of the sky, becoming darker when clouds abound. That, in essence, it is never the same river. Much like people, you tell yourself.

It would be much easier to observe the river from the top of the bridge. But the bridge is a river of people in itself with a ceaseless flow of bodies traversing it at all times of the day. And those people play their music, which is at odds with the music you are searching for. First to the river, yes, but to a quiet enclave where you could meet the waters on your own terms. So, you leave the crowds behind and descend on the island of Kampa, where you follow the greenness of the trees.

There, under the canopy at the edge of the river, you find a quiet place to contemplate the flowing waters. In front of you, the river, inside of you, the flow of conflicted memories and unbridled music. These currents ignore each other, although their mutual influence is undeniable. The surface of the water performs a sinusoidal dance where the valleys and the peaks trade places masquerading the powerful tow of the current underneath. And that is precisely what transpires when you improvise on the violin. The virtuosic notes grab all the attention while the underlying corpus of the melody pushes forward the emotional component of the performance. As for the memories, the moments of gripping fear or ecstatic happiness are easily accessible, while the true essence of what indeed occurred—the emotional scars—travel absconded in the depths of your mind. But you know that sounds tell what really happened, so you listen to the slapping of the water against the rocks and the whispering mist that floats on its surface.

She sang to you often but caressed you rarely. And you still wonder why she opted to touch you with her voice, not her hands or lips. The sound of her voice brought you comfort, but a reserved one, it seems. The few songs you remember were heartfelt and motherly, albeit devoid of warmth. However, those could be ill-formed memories. She may have embraced you dearly and with all the tenderness in the world. Your own disdain for closeness could be distorting and transfiguring those evanescent memories that tend to dissipate as you shed light on them. But that is why you came to the river, to find the trace of her voice and her touch.

You bring the violin out of its case and place it under your chin. With a slow bowing motion, you search for the notes that resemble those of the water as it slaps the rocks. It is not a single note but several. You listen to the rhythmic impulse, to the chords that emanate from the controlled violence of water against rock. Then, you play the resulting natural harmonies and form memories based on them. Those harmonies are yours now. They represent an effort to merge the present sounds with those you may not remember so accurately. Everything sinks inside of you and will resurface later when you play again from the white center of yours.

The river is now behind you. The palpitating heart of a distant youth draws you into the cobblestone streets. You walked on these streets at an age when you had not yet formed a past. The past, that retaining membrane where smells, images and emotions are trapped for later use, was so thin and nubile then. Everything was so fresh and new then; now, everything is so distant. With more reason, thus, you want to expose yourself to the loose murmurs of a past that still floats among the old buildings. Your march brings you to a square impregnated with people and building spires—an intoxicating ambiance rich in sensorial material. Here, you take a chair at an outdoor café and prepare to absorb the various sonic and visual utterances this enclave has to offer.

The wave of people's voices rolls over you. At first, the massive thickness of the sound prevents you from distinguishing the fine details. But as you concentrate on the discrete and individual wavelengths, you begin to hear the nuances. The voice of an old British woman is the first to disturb you, but soon, the voices of Bohemian adolescents drown the voice of the British woman. That makes you feel better. Now, a man of unclear age articulates dubious ideas about beauty and art. You are not convinced, but it does not matter because the delicate voice of a young girl begins to filter into your awareness. You listen to her attentively. What she is talking about, you cannot tell, but you sense that she is happy because of the beautiful dynamics of her sound. The high-pitched vowels descend gradually into a valley of crisp consonants that are so pleasant to the ear. Then, she introduces minute silences that hint at personal discoveries. She reminds you of yourself at a young age to such a degree that you wonder if this is the voice of a nearby girl or the voice of your memories. It does not matter. What matters is that all these voices tickle your sensibility and somehow awaken a sense of the past.

But then you hear him. At first, you are unsure whether it is his voice. Nonetheless, your reaction confirms that it is him talking. First, you sense a paternal warmth with all the security such a voice can convey. It is not the voice of God, for your father was palpable but equally comforting. But soon after, you feel a sense of uneasiness, which makes your blood run cold. You have felt that way before. Your memories contain uneasy visual and cognitive references to malignant actions, gestures, and agency related to your father's image. You look around for the source of the voice. Not surprisingly, men are abundant in this plaza; they comprise all ages, heights, and voice pitches. Any of them could be at the root of what you hear, but at the same time, none of them could elicit the same emotional reaction as your father's voice. Maybe what you hear is not his voice but the echo of his voice. Once your auditory senses register the reality of the surroundings, it begins to resonate inside the chambers of your mind, where it generates an echo. That echo could be the voice you now hear. If that were the case, which of those chambers hide the upsetting memories that distort the sounds? You cannot tell.

Perhaps answers never unravel completely. You may need to content yourself with the crumbs reality throws at you. Better to be alert and receptive to the images and sounds that intercept your life at this moment. Those bits and pieces will percolate through your awareness and reach the magma boiling inside your mind. That magma will need to come out in due time. In the meanwhile, people continue to circulate around the plaza; the spires incline their shadows away from the sun, and the hours parade at a steady rhythm. You rest tranquil, absorbing everything that turns around you until you feel it is time for music to be born.

The crowd, the numerous voices, and the contrasting rhythms all merge and fill you with a destabilizing energy that works against your purpose. You need purity and a clear channel to express your music. So, you walk in haste, looking for the alley that lead you to *AghaRTA* last night. You discard all the improbable passages until the alley eventually appears to your left, from which a musical pulse emerges. That is the way. Behind you, the crowd. Ahead of you is the promise of music as a conduit to the furlong emotions—a frightening proposition, or perhaps an illuminating one—the jazz of your memories.

Deep into the alley, as you approach the luminous sign marking the point of descent, you catch sight of man's silhouette you may recognize. He walks toward you, his face lost in the dark shadows the lamppost behind him fail to illuminate. Instinctively, you turn around to avoid confronting him face-to-face. The man walks around you, ignoring you completely, his gaze focused on the cobblestones as if something was lost among them. He sees you, but he does not see you, an obstacle in a narrow alley you are. Of all possible encounters in this improbable place, why Nicanor? You have no time to answer that question, for there is music to be played.

#

You descend. You sink yourself into the space that fosters expression. Your violin accompanies you, and so does the question of Nicanor. It was Nicanor himself; you are certain of that. But why is he present at the same time and space as you are? You would like to answer that question, but it will distract you from your purpose: to create the music of your memories. So, you decide to put aside such diversion. Let Nicanor do as he wishes. He must have a reason for visiting Prague. You have your own reasons, and that matters more now.

You approach the empty stage and claim your right to play by placing the violin case at the foot of the microphones. Your violin is present, you are present, and your music will assert its presence. The trio of musicians will once again welcome you as they did last night. Why would they do otherwise? You and your violin were honest. Plus, they responded to your extemporary playing and were carried away last night. The four of you played even-tempered music, although you do not share the same memories. And despite your divergent backgrounds, you managed to spend an evening where all of you drank from the same nectar of improvisation. That is what music does; it fosters liaisons among the oddest people.

When the pianist comes into the cave, he instantly recognizes you. He approaches at once but refrains from greeting you. He only asks about your violin, whether you brought it with you. You point to the stage where the violin is anxiously awaiting the opportunity to express itself. He laughs that laughter of his and says that he is ready to listen to you playing nothing. Then he turns his back and walks away to meet someone else behind the stage. This is perfect, exactly what you had hoped for. You have not been repudiated, all the way around, you are expected to play everything.

Why not? A glass of champagne will settle your nerves and help you lift the lid of your memories. And just as you did last night, you make your way to the bar and claim that unraveling glass. However, what rises to the top of your consciousness with the effervescent bubbles are not memories, but the question of Nicanor. Why is Nicanor in Prague? Why was he on the same street as you were? Could it be that he is interested in jazz? Or maybe he is interested in you. That last thought makes you feel uneasy. Perhaps because you barely know him. Yes, you know him, but from a distance, a professional distance. You have listened to almost everything he has composed, and you respect his artistic vision. Although, it is true, you sense that he left behind a few notes in Composition No. 33. But left behind where? If he did not write the notes that you thought should have been written, whose problem is it? How could he be aware that those notes were missing? Because you told him so? Yes, you told him and in so doing perhaps you inflicted some discomfort. He did ask you what those notes were, but you could not have told him for you do not know yourself what those notes are. The question of Nicanor, then, is not why he is in Prague, that is self-evident, but whether he is interested in you as a person, or in you as the source of those missing notes. That is the overhanging question. The glass of champagne, however, does not shed light on any answers.

The audience begins to thicken. People occupy tables, gather at the bar, chat with each other, order their libations, and it impresses you that in preparation for the exercise of listening, they make such a magnanimous noise. You rest serene for you know that tranquility is bound to install itself soon enough. The noise will have to die away and usher in the silence. The first note of your performance will only exist because of the silence that precedes it, but nobody can say with certitude when that silence begins. So, you wait and order a second glass of champagne.

After a while the noise seems to abate somewhat, or perhaps the champagne has softened its edges. It does not matter for what fills you at this moment is the need to embark on the musical journey. This is when the pianist reemerges from behind the stage and gestures to you, an abstruse gesture that you interpret as an invitation. With confidence, you make it to the stage where he has already sat at the piano. With another gesture he summons the drummer and the sax player, both of which spring up from the crowd and come to join you on the stage. They do not seem surprised to see you, on the contrary, it appears as if they were expecting you, as if you have always been an integral part of their group. That is not the case, and you know it, but perhaps they recognize the notes you played last night. Maybe those notes belong to them as much as they belong to you. Or maybe those notes belong to nobody, they could be part of a common sonic memory, the original magma of music.

You open the case and invite your violin onto the stage. It seems anxious, your violin, a resonance arises from its f-holes before you start playing it. It senses your need to express an original sound and it does not want to fail you. You rub its shoulders to help calm it down. Then the pianist plays the "A" note repeatedly and you and the sax player tune to 442 hertz. What follows then is that silence, the one before the first note, a transparent prelude to what is about to unfold.

A thick mist blurs the first image that crosses your mind. All you can identify are shades of green and diffuse light. Music accompanies the image, but you cannot tell whether it is you or the pianist creating the notes. It is probably an old memory that has deteriorated or perhaps a period of your life that lacks clarity. The notes attempt to construct a melody that does not coalesce. The melody meanders loosely about the stage until it extinguishes itself. Unsupported by the music, the image vanishes in turn. After a soft fill played by the drummer,

… you see the image of a young girl grabbing the hand of her mother. They walk in tandem, the girl leading the mother.

And so do the notes that come out of your violin, one after another, tied together in a beautiful legato. The saxophone follows your lead and weaves his notes as well. The melody graciously careens until it reaches the audience. It ascends as high as the vaulted ceiling permits. Then, it turns around and marches back to the stage, one note after another, returning to its origin.

The girl seems to know where she wants to go, the mother follows,

… and the melody clears their path. The pianist nods at you and takes over the control of the melody. He pursues his journey by transposing the melody to the Dorian Mode. You follow him closely, and the saxophone follows you. After a few bars, the pianist reaches the Aeolian Mode, where he rests for a while.

You can still see the girl, but the mother has disappeared at some point during the transposition. Alone, even without a holding hand, the girl seems confident.

The pianist carries further along, folding the melody into a minor harmonic scale. The girl, however, did not make it that far. You do not see her any longer. Maybe she grew older and went on to follow her own music.

Expectant, perhaps insecure, you recede into the background and wait for the other musicians to lead the way. This time, it is the saxophone player who introduces a new theme. Employing his bottom register, he voices a rumbling undertow that flattens you and triggers different memories. *There he is, your father, bearing an unrecognizable face.*

You do not recall what he looked like, but you can still hear his thunderous voice. He never spoke to you directly, perhaps because he did not think you would have understood. But he used the weight of his voice to affect people. At least, that is what your mother must have meant when she said she could not bear the heaviness of his comments. This image triggers a musical response from your right arm. It begins to bow the open G string, producing the lowest possible sound in the violin, the sound at the bottom of the river from where all other sounds spring. Your playing overtakes that of the saxophone and introduces a deep lament that expands within the cavernous space. It is a somber melody looking for a way out of the darkness, a yearning for some overdue repentance. This is not the music you would have chosen to play, but there is an imminent need for its expression. So, you set aside any judgment and play the notes that force their way out of your white center. The piano and the saxophone comprehend your proposed melody's inevitability and play with you. The drummer obliged to respond accordingly, steps hard on the bass drum. After several measures, the image of the unrecognizable face falls over the horizon of your mind where it can no longer be seen. You then bring the melody to an end, and the other musicians follow suit. The music, however, continues to reverberate inside the club for a little longer than you would have desired. When all the notes settle, before stillness has a chance to flood the cave, the pianist gets up from his bench, indicating that a pause is in order. A relief, for you were fearing what the next memory could unleash.

#

To avoid the need to explain your music, you step away from the stage and seek refuge in a dark corner from where you can observe the crowd without having to interact with it. You are not afraid of people, no, you are not, but you are afraid of having to share with people the nebulous source of your inspiration, although, inspiration may not be exactly what propels you to play those notes. Those images could be memories, but you cannot recall the events attached to them. Perhaps these are mere constructs of your mind as it tries to settle uneasy moments of your past. But does the past really exist even when you have no recollection of it? Maybe it does, hidden away in those dark rooms of your mind where the light of consciousness has yet to penetrate.

People in the audience become restless; they move around the cave as if in desperate need of relief. They go back and forth to the bar, around the stage, up and down the stairs to the entrance. Maybe they need to shake off the heaviness of the last song. They could also be anxious for more music. Or perhaps they are not anxious at all, and it is only the projection of your own insecurities. But what is there to be insecure about? You master your instrument, you have a complete command of the musical form, and you blend perfectly well with the other musicians. That is all well, however, you have yet to allow for your emotional response to those memories and the melodies they elicit. In due time you will, but this moment right now is for exploration and release.

And as you are having these thoughts, you notice a distinctive silhouette moving through the crowd. This image is not a memory, but the veritable figure of Nicanor who meanders thru the cave with an air of urgency. After fumbling around, he finds an empty chair right in front of the stage and takes root there. When you saw him earlier in the alley, he appeared discombobulated, now he seems alert and intent on confronting something. That something could be you, or perhaps not you as an individual, but your music. At the same time, he could have descended into this cave by mere chance, a proposition you find hard to believe.

Let the shadows protect you; let the anonymity shield you for the moment. But you know this pause will soon end because the other musicians will request your presence on the stage. You ignited their playing, and they will certainly want to hear more from you. They do not need to know that you are playing your personal history, even if that history is fragmented and barely recognizable to you. Most likely, each of them is playing their own history as well. And as such, your individual histories are intertwined in the process of improvising. The four of you may be plural as individuals, but the ensemble of your music is singular.

In the dark corner you remain, uncertain of what images may come to visit you and what melodies they will call forth. Your violin rests on the stage, impatient. It does not know what it will be asked to execute. You are impatient as well and would love another glass of champagne which could only be obtained at the bar. To reach the bar means to expose yourself to the dim lights of the club and risk being approached by people, maybe Nicanor himself. So, you rest immobile, in anticipation, hoping for time to traverse time. You wait, and you wait some more. An impossibility, for you cannot kill time without injuring eternity. Thus, you spring up from the dark corner and storm the stage. You pick up your violin and begin to bow the strings, your mind open, your eyes closed.

The drummer, intent on not missing a step, joins you on the stage and molds a groove around your playing. He does not anticipate; he follows you at a safe distance while trying to understand the images you are conjuring. But you have a hard time discerning a clear image from the reverie that floods your mind. You see a diffuse parade of possibilities where no single image asserts control. Your playing, then, threatens to break apart the loose melodic line you have managed to weave together. This is when you open your eyes. And when you get used to the glare of the spotlights, you realize that Nicanor is sitting right in front of you with his eyes closed. Can he not afford to look at you, or is the erratic music transporting him to an erratic place in his mind? It does not matter, for you are not here because of him. On the other hand, he may be here because of you, and in such a case, the images that count are those reposing deep in your memory well.

You close your eyes again. The sound of your violin begins to organize itself. Soon the piano contributes a few tentative notes. The saxophone then injects some color to the shifting melody.

In front of your mind's eye materializes the image of a vast sea, unending, almost blue, with ripples on its back caused by a runaway wind. So ample this sea that it threatens to drown your music. No point in trying to contain it, so you throw yourself into its body. You sink deep into it. And the deeper you sink, the more luminous it becomes and the clearer the sound of your violin.

What you are now playing is the pure essence of who you are, that which is unfiltered, a melody straddling two land masses, Bohemia, and that island of hers. The piano recognizes your plea and offers you a warm support while the saxophone weaves a reassuring melody between your notes. Then you hear the waves breaking and the clamor of cymbals as you and your violin emerge from the surf.

The meaning of your improvisation is not accessible to the audience, but there is a clear sense that a rupture has taken place. Thus, the applause and the bravos. The pianist nods at you and laughs while the drummer claps with his wooden sticks. You do not know what you just played. The notes have already vanished as well as the images that gave them birth. Nothing remains, only the memory of having touched deep memories, the kind that give rise to a personal music in search of understanding.

You would prefer not to acknowledge Nicanor's presence, but his position in the first row of tables is unsurmountable. You focus your gaze on the very back of the room where people's faces are bathed in shadows. They may have learned something about you by means of your playing, but you do not know who they are. Then you look toward the bar, the source of champagne, where people are half-clapping with a cigarette in one hand and a half-full glass in the other, a gassy crowd that is. The weight of obligation then forces you to focus on Nicanor's face. It is him, there is no doubt. He remains impassive with his eyes closed. You cannot ascertain what he experienced by listening to your playing. You wonder if he even creates music like you do, in response to what resides in the deep white center. Perhaps the vacuum you have found in his composition results from his reticence to visit those dark chambers of the mind. Or maybe he just cannot see.

The pianist introduces the saxophone player to the audience. He must be well known by the regulars for they clap with enthusiasm. He then presents the drummer, a younger player still trying to assert his position in the trio. But his youth does not detract from his talent and the audience seems to appreciate him wholeheartedly. The pianist will now introduce you. You do not know what he will say. He knows you are a violin player that comes from somewhere else. But he does not know the true nature of your music, where it comes from, nor what it means to you. Not surprisingly, you pose to yourself the same questions. He begins by announcing your name pronounced with an accent sounding like that of your father, if your memory does not betray you. He then says that you are here for unknown reasons but that it is evident you can play everything and nothing. The audience celebrates the awkward introduction with a round of applause. This applause, or perhaps the mentioning of your name, derails Nicanor's evasive meditation for he opens his eyes and focuses his gaze on you. You accept the confrontation and gaze directly back at him. However, this communion offers no clarification. You do not really know what he thinks nor the reason for his presence in this underground cave. At the same time, he knows not your motivations for playing outside of the classical canon, nor the source of your inspiration. Despite these discrepancies, something is being shared.

Alone, without consulting with the other musicians, you begin to play your violin again. They seem to trust your lead and inventiveness for they stay quiet and allow you to pursue an unexpected solo. Your violin trusts you as well and follows your lead in searching for old forgotten notes. At this point your mind is a blank slate and every melody is possible. The memories will soon arise, and so will the music. But until the inner magma begins to boil, the Utopia of your music will not be accessible to you. And without Utopia creativity is not possible.

Then he speaks, Nicanor, directing his words at you from his preferential first row. He begs you to play the missing notes. After thus speaking, he closes his eyes again and recedes into his mind. The notes he is asking for do not belong to you, and they will only resurface if the creative process has a need for them. So, you launch yourself into the abyss of improvisation in the hopes of touching a piece of Utopia.

What am I afraid of? Why do I have to avoid a mystifying confrontation? If it is indeed Neva who is playing tonight, was not the sort of serendipity I had expected? I came to Prague for a reason, and now when the reason is about to manifest, I abort the process. No, I cannot allow such idiocy. So, I stop my fugitive march in the middle of this narrow alley. The club is only about a hundred meters behind me. All I must do is turn around, retrace my steps, and descend once more into that cave where I will confront my own purpose.

But what is my urgency? Shall I not allow for time to take its time? If I were to rush into the bowels of that cave and assert my presence as if it were a gift from some god, would that not alter the natural development of the very essence I am pursuing? It certainly would. So, I do turn around but proceed at a ridiculously slow pace in the direction of the mouth that will swallow me and digest my expectations. Anyone watching my seemingly arduous advance would take me for a cripple. I may be crippled, but not physically. Mentally, perhaps, but no, not mentally in the sense of capacity or sharpness, but certainly in the realm of memory interpretations. That is where I feel like an imbecile. Enough self-torture… let me forge ahead.

After slowly dragging myself through the alley, I finally arrive at the entrance of the *AghaRTA* where I can barely discern what is being played down in the cave. I hear the unmistakable voice of a violin recounting a story unknown to me. At first the violin sings alone, then it is joined by the piano and the saxophone. But those two instruments do not expand the narrative, they just support the story being told. Then the sound quivers, it loses its power and becomes rather thin, almost disappearing in the mist of the street noise. Then it builds its presence again, this time introducing a new story. But all I get to hear are fragments of those stories, like when somebody whispers a secret that has died a little.

What now follows is a complete absence of music creating a void which is immediately filled by the clapping of hands and the rumbling of human voices. The musicians are now silent, placing the narrative in a sort of suspense. I feel embolden by the possibility of gliding into the cave in complete anonymity without having to impose my presence. So, I descend slowly, hoping that confronting my own purpose would do me no harm. When I reach the bottom of the stairs, I come to face a compact mass of bodies, allowing little room for maneuvering. I look for a place to hide, to abstract my presence from the boiling audience. But every nook inside the cave contains a body, leaving me no option but to be out in the open. There, in the open, I see a table without glasses on top of it, and an empty chair as a companion. Their appearance is languid, and I feel as if they are calling to me. I should resist the call, but I do not, for there may be a memory of this table and chair hidden somewhere in my mind. So, I walk over and take possession of the space. And in so doing, I find myself right in front of the stage, facing the music about to re-emerge.

I retreat into my own self. Although I want to absorb the music that is about to happen, I fear it may impact me with a brutal force. But here I am, right in front of the stage. The only barrier between the music and my ears is a rather thin air. I close my eyes and travel deep inside my mind seeking refuge. I will listen from the inside of one of those empty chambers where a faint echo of the music will come to meet me.

One of the musicians presents the members of the ensemble. His masculine voice comes from the left of the stage. He must be the pianist. He speaks with the reposed conviction of someone who is satisfied with himself. He must be the leader of the group, but perhaps not the most talented. He mentions two names that have no meaning to me. Then he speaks her name—Neva. Yes, I am hearing her name. I was expecting to hear her name, but I was not expecting for her to stand in front of me. Leaving the empty chamber of my mind, I force my way out in the open. I step forward and open my eyes, confirming that Neva is indeed standing on the stage, her intense eyes gazing at me.

She dives into the music, alone, as if an immediate need to express something personal propels her fingers. The other musicians hold back and allow her to take flight. What she plays bears no resemblance to any music I have ever written. This is raw and intimate, something she values for its private meaning. Transfixed, she traverses scales, wielding improbable notes and proposing silences. She plays with a purpose, and I wonder what that purpose is. I need to know, for in knowing, I may find more about myself. So, I burst into spoken language and ask her to play the missing notes she unearthed from Composition No. 33. I regret my abrupt utterance at once. I know not, but I may have broken a spell. I feel exposed and inappropriate. So, I close my eyes again and disappear inside one of those dusty rooms of my mind.

What she plays next is extraordinary. The notes assemble themselves in pictorial ways. They begin to depict images I have not visualized in ages.

There I am, a child again, in front of a marble lion who struggles to release itself from the powerful embrace of a serpent—one predator confronting another in the ultimate duel, the one for existence. I can see the brutal animality of the encounter. I can hear the rapid breath of the lion under the silent clutch of the serpent's body. Then the lion roars, and so does the violin. But the serpent's crush breaks his ribs, and he roars no longer. Only the sibilant stream of air surging from the serpent's lungs can now be heard. Or perhaps it is the harmonics of the E string from Neva's violin that I hear.

This I see without seeing, for my eyes are closed. My memories, however, come forth and propose one representation after another, wanting to align me with the extemporaneous playing Neva unleashes inside this Bohemian cave.

One of those memories begins to undulate right in front of my eyes. It bears no image, it represents nothing. It looks more like a wave of light that travels through the dense air of the cave. It first assumes a harmless flat profile before beginning to twist into crests and troughs. The wave then acquires a frightening amplitude producing a pulsation that resonates deep inside my body. I can feel the cadence, the call from a time before this time. What I see is not the shape of music but the contours of a culture I have long ignored. Classical rhythm is broken, syncopation reigns in its place.

My mind wants to see more, but the parade of memories comes to an end when the other musicians overwhelm Neva's solo with a deluge of uninspired notes. They want to contribute. They want to be heard. I understand. Consequently, they snap the cordon of intertwined memories that joined Neva's music and my mind. The leveled field is ravaged. We may be in front of each other, but I no longer see or hear the pulse of her inner music. I am not sure what kind of music she played. Clearly, she did not play the missing notes from Composition No. 33.

I can remain just where I am and continue to marvel at her virtuosity. I can encourage the procession of memories to continue deep into the night. I can also forget the reasons that brought me here and enjoy the music for music's sake. I could also forget that I am a composer and aliment my hunger with nubile melodies and syncopated rhythms. But that is a tall order. My reality wants to assert itself and look for a logical order within the realm of the received. I want to fight that tendency, especially now that I find myself in front of such an ardent pulse. But my strength is insufficient. I need to hold back my instincts and shake away the grip of fear. Did not I come here on my own account? Yes, I did.

When a server comes by my table, I implore for a first glass of wine. Any color—red, white, rosé—it does not matter. If I were a blind man, the color of wine would be virtually inconsequential. Likewise, with my eyes shot, the music detaches itself from each of the individual musicians. What I hear is a general yearning, and what I see is the projection of my memories. Let the wine enter my body. Let the music exhume the broken toys of my youth. Let Neva experiment with this extraneous language that rebels against the canon, my canon that is, the one that has bent my neck.

#

I feel a rupture about to happen. There is no sense in looking for cover since I cannot hide from my own self. I must allow this music to traverse me. Perhaps a few notes will take residence inside my mind. They should not be afraid, these notes, for the ones that already exist inside my mind will accommodate the newcomers. After all, they are all children of the same divinity. However, I should not underestimate the potential disarray this opening can create. But I must relax and be permissive for chaos could be a creative force.

The notes unleash a whirlwind. I no longer hear the

music the ensemble is playing. I no longer see the faded pictures of things past. I feel like I have swallowed a small universe that wants to expand inside of me. All the notes clamor at the same time, vibrating in unison, creating a basso continuo that reverberates throughout the depths of my core. At the same time, the images of all the memories have coalesced engendering a diffuse white light that shines peacefully. This must be the essence, the magma.

With my eyes still closed, I get up from the table. I trudge away from the stage, like a blind man, feeling tables and people with my hands until I make it all the way to the bar. The server asks if there is something wrong with me. I ask for him to direct me toward the exit. He turns my body around and gives me a gentle push in the back. I trudge some more and make it to the stairs. I begin to climb, and as I ascend, the sound of the violin falls away from me.

Once again, I inhabit the narrow alley that leads toward or away from the *AghaRTA*. This time, I walk away from the club, but not as the same person that entered it just a little while ago. I have heard, and I have seen. Neva had something to say. She played her music, which was not intended to influence me. Then, my memories unleashed an assault on me that was not necessarily linked to the music Neva was playing. Or perhaps there was a link, but I cannot ascertain what that could have been. All this taking place inside the bowels of this ancient town that has harbored the past of countless generations, native and otherwise. Would I have come to this town if I had not visited it before? Is the direct experience of a place necessary to bring forth buried images from the past? Could we rely on the power of our mind to evoke sounds and pictures of times past while in the surroundings of a sterile present? More precisely, do we have to travel physically to arrive at the early stages of our emotional experience?

Let me walk fast, let me not think so much. I traverse old streets where young people gather to celebrate their youth. The same old streets contain old people who celebrate their wisdom, albeit in a more solitary way. The streets have no agency of their own, they exert their impact indirectly, by means of the imagination. We are who we are, and we project out to the world that which we wish to be. The old streets serve as a backdrop without which our real or imaginary existence would disintegrate. At such a fast pace I cross the old bridge and start climbing toward the old castle. This must be a known ritual, the ascension to higher ground after a complicated excursion inside the bowels of the underworld.

At the turn of a corner, I come across a man and his dog, both sitting on the floor, the man with a guitar, the dog with no bone to gnaw on. They seem like children of a distracted god, the man dressed in rags and the dog sporting matted fur. Their solitude is remarkable considering the ebullience of this town. My first instinct is to walk around them and continue my ascent, for I get a sense of devastation and hopelessness when witnessing misery, especially when I have no power to correct it. But a few notes from the guitar make me slow down and listen attentively. The man has not realized that I am listening, and neither has the dog lifted an eye. He is playing for himself and his companion, music that must soothe them both. A sort of ballad, poetry perhaps, in words that resemble Spanish. And that is precisely what captures my attention, the authenticity. Each note is a testament, a reflection of the soul of this poor man, expertly played without pretension.

I feel the urge to interrupt him and inquire about the song, but I refrain myself. Let him carry on unaffected by my curiosity. After all, this is his music, and I am of no consequence to him. So, I stand at a distance but close enough to listen to every single note. From where I am, I try to ascertain what sort of expression has fallen on the man's face. I see a stare, not a hard one, but coolly focused on the cobblestones in front of him. That is his tabula rasa, the surface where his music lands. He cares not if people step over his music, for it has already been played and soothed his soul.

When the song comes to an end, the dog whimpers and turns its body around while the man lifts his gaze from the cobblestones. He searches the surroundings, perhaps looking for human contact or hoping to hide away from it. Inevitably, he stumbles upon my gaze, and there he rests. His expression is essentially neutral: relaxed almond-shaped eyes, high cheekbones, and lips without inflection, all these features framed by black hair cascading down to his shoulders. I wonder how such a heartfelt song could have emerged from a seemingly dispassionate man. However, I must accept that a face may not always be the mirror of the soul.

I feel the uneasy weight of his stare and impassivity. He reveals no obligation to speak to me and no urgency to initiate any action. He is sitting in the company of his dog, and he has already played his music. It is up to me to respond, for I have apprehended his expression and offered none in return. So, I venture to ask the basest of questions: I enquire about the meaning of the song I just heard. The man does not react, nor does he answer my question. He simply continues to stare at me without curiosity, as if he had not heard a single word I spoke. I reconsider my situation and comprehend that I am an intruder. I walked into the intimate world of this man and his dog and drank from a nectar that did not belong to me. Ashamed of my behavior, I turn my back on them and continue my walk toward the castle. But after only a few steps, I hear the man's voice behind me. The words that I hear are clearly in Spanish this time. The tone of his voice is surprisingly tender. For an instant, I consider forging ahead in my walk. But I do not. Why would I ignore that which is authentic?

I turn around and retrace my steps coming as close to this man as I feel comfortable. Now standing tall, he still regards me with the same inscrutable expression while the dog ignores me completely. I remain quiet and wait for him to speak again. A couple of people turn the same corner I did just a moment ago and threaten to interrupt our exchange. But they hear no music and continue with their march. The street is now silent, like a hollow cathedral when nobody is praying. So here we remain, this man, his guitar, and his dog, one in front of each other, without saying a single word.

While still gazing at me, he pets his dog on the head and picks up his guitar. He then starts to strum a gentle melody. The notes, as tender as his voice, begin to circle around me. I accept them, I listen to them, and I try to decipher their meaning. A personal meaning that is, for what other meaning could a melody have but the one instilled by the ears that welcome it? And my ears do welcome this melody. At first it appears unrelated to me, but it soon begins to evolve, to turn around itself, and to reach deep into my mind. There, inside the vastness, the melody reverberates at ease, eliciting a peaceful sensation that is as authentic as any of my memories. And the more I listen, the more the melody rings familiar. And the more familiar it rings, the closer it comes to the sound of that fugitive melody of mine.

This man knows not who I am, nor does he know about what is missing—melodies, memories, or what have you. He cannot be part of my universe. Although, I must admit that the universe is wider than my views of it. Regardless of whether this man and I share anything in common, he is playing the melody I have failed to capture. Or at least that is what I think he is playing. Once again, I feel the urge to interrupt him, to steal this melody from him. But the instant I shift my attention from my tumultuous thoughts to his playing, what I hear is the silence of a hollow cathedral.

Nobody is singing and nobody is praying. The melody has vanished.

Here we stand, the man holding on to his guitar while I am holding on to my uneasiness, both facing each other with his dog as the only witness to this encounter. Although he seems to be at complete peace with himself, a loud disquiet grows inside of me. Once again, I reach for answers and ask him for the name of the song he just played. And I regret at once having asked the question, not because he may ignore the question as he already did before, but because he may answer it, in which case I would have to deal with the consequences. The few seconds that follow contain nothing but a silence that burns me. Or perhaps what burns is the weight of my shame, I cannot tell. At some point in time, he bends down to whisper something to his dog, his confidant. He then straightens his body, faces me, and tells me that he does not know the name of the song nor its origin. Or at least that is what I understand he says for he mumbles his words. I offer him a smile, not because I feel any joy or happiness, but because he is clearly being honest. He then carries on talking and what I can gather are fragments of understanding. He says that he plays what comes to his heart, that the songs come and go, that this song must have come along with me when I turned that corner, that his dog can smell an air of tension around me.

I dare not ask any further questions. I dare not listen to any more music. This man is part of my experience today, an experience that may be linked to prior experiences that continue to escape me. Regardless of the reason for his existence, let me turn around and walk away from this man before the stench of my tension suffocates his dog and unsettles my mind any further. Up the hill I go at a rapid pace, toward the castle, toward an improbable peace. What inner peace could there be if what I am looking for out in the world is indeed inside of me, wrapped in layers of memories, and somehow only discernible by sensible musicians or a matted hound.

#

From the window of my hotel room, I can see the universe. It offers itself to me in the shape of red roofs, black spires, and rolling hills. It contains my life now and my life then. All the music that was ever composed, whether it was written or not, is also contained within that universe. If I were to put my hand through the window's glass, I would be able to grab the entirety of that universe. There would be blood, but that is irrelevant. If I were to hold the universe in my hands, I would be able to peel its historical layers and arrive at those critical moments of my past. As I am having these thoughts, a grayish brume mounts an assault on the hill, and the universe is no longer. That is how quickly our hopes disappear. One second everything seems possible, and the next only evanescence.

I know the melody exists in that universe, that is now evident to me. In my pursuit, however, the melody seems to pursue me, for it tends to invade the spaces I inhabit. Perhaps it is the melody that wants something from me, and not the reverse. Maybe it needs to be heard and appreciated, or maybe it has something to reveal. If there were to be a message hidden in that melody, it would likely be a personal one. The guitar player did not react emotionally to his own playing, neither does Neva react when she improvises and spills out those notes I am trying to assemble. The one that becomes transfixed when listening to that fugitive melody is only myself. This is a personal quandary.

Outside the window the brume continues to flood the visual field. I keep quiet and try to listen for unintentional sibilance, whispers, or any other sound the brume would emit on its passage. But I hear nothing, a quiet brume this is. Maybe the brume is like our memories, it engulfs our visual field in utter silence, and we are left alone to compose the music of our reveries.

If the music that taunts me is the music of my past, and if my past is somehow intertwined with Neva and the narrow alleys of this old town, I should be able to find its traces. Music is bound to leave traces, either as emotional carcasses hidden inside deep rooms of our mind, or as ephemeral vibrations hovering over the roofs and spires of old towns like this one. What is clear to me is that sitting at my desk and attempting to compose music that is true to myself will lead to failure and disappointment. I reject such a fate. I must sample the wind and distill the brume with the hope of extracting those evasive notes.

Most of the music I have heard in my formative years remains in my brain in the form of a seed. As soon as it is watered by attention, the seed tends to germinate at once in full splendor. On the other hand, the music linked to my past is rather ephemeral and shies away from me upon a fleeting look. Maybe it does not want to be heard again, or maybe it fears I would react adversely if I were to take it deep into my conscience. But I should be the master of my musical universe even if it contains disturbing elements that could be sinister. What is there to fear, except myself?

This task requires all able hands on the ship. I will tackle it with my open mind, but I will bring my sound recorder since my mind could play tricks on me by allowing notes to escape when they feel threatened. The mind has a mind of its own, and we may never know what that other mind thinks. To prepare myself, I start by looking out of the window. Perfect, the brume has not cleared out. It is all there, in complete plenitude and grayness. I tuck the sound recorder under my arm. Then I appease my mind by thinking of Neva's playing, her lucidity, her candor. I tell myself that this is a quest for the truth of my musical past, inevitable, even if fugacious. And thus armed, I burst out into the streets.

In this late hour, I am received by darkness and no applause. The streets care little for my intrusion. They were here before me and will continue to exist once I have departed. But these same streets are the silent witnesses of everything that has occurred within their confines. Their memory is not an organic one, like mine. Theirs is made of brick and stone, and for that reason less emotional. Those hard surfaces only need to reflect the sufferance of people like me who walk with trepidation at the possibility of remembering something disagreeable. Regardless of this reality, I venture through the streets.

After descending for a few blocks, I come to a plaza where a church stands tall, projecting an intimidating presence that must have previously served a wicked purpose. A futile effort today, for many bars and restaurants line the plaza and look directly at the church without intimidation. A timeless battle in a place of conflict suits my needs. Yes, many words must have been spoken and many chants released to the sky in this very plaza. However, only a few people frequent these surroundings late at night. Maybe the shadows, or a latent fear... I cannot tell. An arcade provides the perfect place from where I can stand and watch the open space while keeping abreast of the shadows behind me. I can be seen, but only so slightly. I then prepare the microphone and turn on the sound recorder. I keep silent, I even try not to breathe. The sounds that I need are not the ones inside of me, but those that circulate freely and bounce from one ancient wall to another.

At some point I hear steps across the plaza, the nervous laughter of a young woman, a conversation between two dilapidated men, the wheels of a slow car, the echo of a sound I cannot identify, the silence of the church bells, the dog that refuses to obey, the faint buzz of accumulated expectation as if something is about to happen. Amid the anomalous sounds, the image of my young self materializes at the entrance of the church.

That is me at the steps, by the tall door, looking inside that temple of fear. I'm drawn inside the church by a sense of duty or perhaps by the illusion that something beyond my pedestrian life could be found there. And I didn't know, and nobody told me, so what could I do or say? Not the voices of angels. They are dead already. What I'm hearing is the sound of a Misa Criolla where percussion rouses the demons. I listen with my eyes closed because the view of the priest and the cross are too saintly for what the music proposes. Let it rip, rip it apart. The music does not listen to the church, and the church does not listen to the music, and me in the middle wondering, why?

I already lost my religion, so what I am seeing must be an old memory wanting to come out of hiding. Maybe the memory needs to be heard. Perhaps it knows that I am in the process of recording and hope to be immortalized. I always thought that I had an inherent need for memories as if life would not be complete in their absence. But I never considered that memories might have needs of their own which we systematically repress because to acknowledge such a powerful inner world could weaken the sense of sovereignty over our minds. The question is: what happens after a memory expresses itself in such a flagrant way? Do other memories follow on their own account? Or is it me who unconsciously welcomes them, hoping to elicit the lost music of my youth? Actually, does it matter how any of this happens?

Another image lands on the forefront of my awareness…

That is me kneeling in front of a wooden pew, the saintly wooden images hanging from an impossible ceiling that has no end. Next to me, my comrades, kneeling as well, in a sort of trance. Their arms raised, their tongues turning and twisting, uttering incomprehensible sounds. Not their language, but that of a god through them. Or perhaps a song that emanates from their inner fear of having sinned, as if a young boy would know how to sin purposely. The endless ceiling collects the sounds and offers no echo. What is said, what is sung, leaves a thin trace in our collective unconscious, or perhaps no trace at all. But I listen as I see, and I see myself listening.

Then comes the wind, fostering chaos and disarray. Not a cold wind, but a humid one, a partner of the brume, it seems. It blows away the notes, the words, and even the loose images that were already somewhat unhinged. I am left with a sense of emptiness as if my efforts to recuperate those particles of my past were inevitably cut short. But the wind is not a formidable opponent, even though I know not what it looks like or where it comes from. The wind always dies down; it has no other option. And that is exactly what happens. After unleashing numerous gusts, the invisible force vanishes and leaves a trail of stillness in its wake. There is no longer a child at the door of the church, and no chant comes from its entrails. I now see the lonely silhouette of a stone building surrounded by timid shadows that project their long bodies in all directions. What I now hear is quietude.

Satisfied with having recorded some melodic samples,

I dispense with the protection of the arcade and begin to climb back toward the castle. I am not sure what kind of music I captured, but it must be linked to those images of my past. Provided, of course, that those images represent real events of my past and not merely distorted memories that fail to recall any truth. I will never be able to know for sure since there are no means of corroboration. But I did record the *Misa Criolla* and the twisted utterances of my comrades. I have possession of those sounds, and the moment I get to replay them, the images will come alive in my mind's eye once more.

When I turn the same corner that earlier brought me face-to-face with the guitar player and his dog, I am assaulted by the fear that a difficult encounter is about to happen. The space, however, is completely empty and nothing indicates that a man sang songs with his guitar or that a dog gnawed at no bone. What remains of that encounter is only a memory. Let it be that way for I have more tangible material to deal with.

Once inside the hotel room, I come to stand in front of the window. I can see the town peacefully sleeping on its back. The red roofs and the black spires are still there as a testament to the persistence of time. The brume, although fluid and ephemeral in nature, still floats languidly as congealed time. Nothing other than my own sense of a conflicted past seems to have changed. I place the sound recorder on the small night table next to the bed. I press the play button and turn toward the window to continue admiring the long night outside. I wait to hear the melody of my past, of lost religion, and lost comrades. I wait for notes that may point in the direction of that which is missing. But all I hear is the sound of the wind that refuses to die down this time.

You played what needed to be played. How the music impacted Nicanor, you cannot ascertain, for he is no longer at the table in front of the stage. Maybe you did not play what he asked you to play, but you never play what people ask you to play while improvising. Playing the music written by others is a different story. Perhaps that is what Nicanor wanted, for you to play the music he already wrote. But it seems he was probably asking for you to play what he failed to write. But you do not have full command of those notes, yet he is not aware of that.

The night goes on; the music goes on. You put aside the vision of Nicanor and continue to play what erupts from inside. The other musicians follow you at times. At other times, they bring forth their own memories, and you follow them in turn. The conversation twists and turns in seemingly random ways, and the audience seems to comprehend, for they applaud at every solo and cheer when virtuosity is on display. And so, the night glides until the pianist announces the final piece, which all of you play enthusiastically, bringing the performance to an end.

But the end of the performance only heralds the beginning of what is about to happen. The mass exodus of the audience leaves behind an emptiness that resonates with power in the voluminous void. A sense of anticipation hangs in the air as if a miracle were to take place at any moment. In the depths of the cave vacated by the public, the other musicians finish a most-needed drink and keep utterly silent. Then, one by one, the pianist, the sax player, and the drummer go back on the stage. You do not know what they intend to do, but if music is to be born again, you want to be part of the experience. And before you finish this very thought, the pianist asks what is taking you so long and requests that you join them on the stage.

The four of you are there, facing each other, not playing a single note. You break the silence by speaking, thanking them for allowing you to play tonight. The pianist interrupts you at once and says there is nothing to say with words and that nobody is allowed to use those symbols. He then returns to the silence and urges you to pick up your violin by nodding his head. You comprehend. Words are burdened by meaning, and they often fail to jolt our imagination. Words are the symbols we use when music is not at hand. So, you pick up your violin and bow the strings in the most thankful way you can fashion. You hope they understand your appreciation by means of the music alone. Your eyes are shut, your face impassive. When you stop playing, the pianist laughs that laugh of his and prompts you to continue. What then follows is not the music of appreciation but the music of remembrance, for, at this moment, you feel like a young girl striding two disparate worlds that coincided by pure chance. The higher notes paint your memories with ebullient colors, fearless, facing a sun that knows no retreat. On the contrary, the lower notes imbue your memories with a grayish tonality, like that of mist under the shadows of a lonesome tree. You play until you have nothing else to say. Then you open your eyes.

The saxophone player takes over and blows an array of notes that reveal his days as a difficult adolescent. You can sense how he walks on the edge of danger, consuming substances that confuse brain cells and unveil unknown dimensions. He climbs high, higher than he could even envision. From that plenitude he falls abruptly to the stone floor and the notes splash against the walls and the dirty glasses that remain on the empty tables. You do not know this young man, but you know that he has played with fire, and his inner music wants to tell you that story. Then he renders a less dynamic melody, soft and velvety, as if peace could be had on this earth, as if repentance were valid.

The drummer wants to say something. You know, because he bobs his head while twirling the mallets between his fingers. Lifetime memories seem to be elapsing through him. And once the saxophone player's last melancholy note expires, the drummer erupts into a controlled frenzy. He is rhythmic, precise, and time-obedient. But the straight jacket of his groove reveals a desire for alterity. Now, when the grove becomes thinner, he introduces syncopated hits that want to break the mold and threaten to venture into a different rhythmic path. But this urge is aborted, for he quickly reins in his impulses and returns to the original groove. You understand his dilemma: to run away or to abide.

The natural order of things would be for the pianist to embark on his own journey. Instead, he closes the fallboard of the piano and begins to whistle a simple melody. So familiar this melody, so different from what the others were playing, perhaps so intimate to you. Why did your mother have to go? Why did she abandon him? Or was it he who sent her away? Or the Cuban government, did they want her back? You do not know. And this is why you are here because you want to know. The answers, however, are not abundant. They shy away from you, and they disappear in the mist. So, you interrupt the pianist to ask him what song he is now whistling. He reminds you not to use words and that nobody is allowed to use those symbols.

Everyone had the chance to express what they wanted, but different from the earlier performance, these were individual expressions born from the idiosyncratic realities of each musician. How do you respond to the sound of danger, to the rhythm of desire, to the whiteness of a whistle? With notes of your own? Perhaps… But how could you visualize the images that engendered those melodies and sounds? You simply cannot. You need words to complement the partial understanding. But words are not allowed at this time. In essence, you must accept that not everything is attainable and that reality contains lacunae that will always remain obscure. Yet, you have the desire to find out more, to comprehend better, to visualize a clearer picture of those memories that dance in front of your mind's eye.

Silence makes a majestic return and reigns supreme inside the cave. The absence of music is followed by the absence of words. The other musicians seem comfortable with this arrangement, and you do your best to emulate them. Your right hand, however, wants to bow the violin strings and speak loudly. But you control yourself because you are the outsider, the one who just arrived, the one who does not know. And such expressive restraint opens another channel, that of your buried memories…

He does not say goodbye, and he does not look back when you and your mother stand there on the train platform with your makeshift suitcases. He simply walks away. When the train arrives, your mother drags you inside a cabin. You stand on the bench and look out the window. He is not there any longer.

Someone turns off the stage lights. A signal, it seems, that the seance is over. The pianist leads the way down to the bar, inviting everyone to a drink. You ask for a glass of champagne. The others get a Pilsner. They raise their glasses as if they were going to toast, but nobody says a word. Instead, they look at you in anticipation. You are the new arrival, and the burden is on you to illuminate the moment.

The truth is that you have nothing else to say. You have already expressed yourself by means of your violin. On the other hand, they could tell you things you want to know. But it seems wiser not to ask questions now; that is not what they expect. So, you decide to congratulate them on their fine playing and their improvisational skills. And you are being sincere because they played extremely well. Their facial expressions, a mixture of disbelief and equivocal surprise, tell you that that was not what they expected you to say either. The pianist then says that you played your "every-thing," as you had promised earlier, but that they did not get to hear your "nothing." The sax player and the drummer nod in agreement. You respond by saying that, in your impression, both the sax player and the drummer also played their "everything" and that nothing was left behind. The pianist quickly retorts, insisting that "nothing" was indeed left behind, that it needs to be rescued. Yes, it needs to be rescued since "nothing" is not available to you. What you play is a mere echo of what you remember. There is more; you just do not know what it is or where to find it.

Then the pianist laughs that laughter of his again and adds that some harmonies in your playing remind him of people he has known in the past but that he is not sure who they could be. And you are sure he will not reveal much if you were to ask him for clues, so you do not. From this moment on, once the alcohol has worked its magic, the conversation follows another current. There is mention of the future of jazz, the need for caves like this one to subsist, whether musical consciousness has a mind of its own, or whether the music of the self is nothing other than the random vibrations of brain cells. Nothing that is discussed is personal. Everything collapses into the realm of nothingness.

On the way up the stairs, once the club is about to enter its dormant stage, the pianist whispers to you that he will whistle again tomorrow, to meet him at the door of the club at high noon. You hold your breath and whisper nothing in return.

You have nothing to lose. Or perhaps you have everything to lose and nothing to gain. The early morning proposes no solutions; it only offers the opportunity for you to decide how to proceed. The morning knows it will have to capitulate by noon, at which time you would either be opening a door into a potentially uncomfortable unknown or walking away in fear. Regardless of any decision you make, you still wonder why the pianist whistled to you. He could have played the same melody on the keyboard but chose to whistle instead. A whistling sound is nothing but wind under pressure, moving fast through a narrow space, yielding a nearly pure tone. But there was something personal in his gesture. The air came from within himself, and the narrow space was created by his pursed lips. Purity, perhaps, or tenderness...

What holds you back is not a fear of the melody he played but of his commentary about your own music. He mentioned a connection with people he has known in the past. How could your playing be associated with phantoms he cannot even identify? Or can he? He is a relatively old man, so his past must be deep and wide. He must have met many people and listened to many melodies. There must be a legion of phantoms inside his mind. But, somehow, he made a link between you and some of them. And that is the reason for your sudden visit to Prague. Yes, it is, so you need not fear the pianist. On the contrary, you should approach him unarmed, without your violin, with your ears and mind open. If he were to whistle again, you would listen attentively for any recognizable and familiar notes in the music. If it happens that your mind presents you with uneasy images of your childhood, you should confront them without judgment. After all, the image of the self is only an image, and the feelings of harshness and tenderness are only feelings. They are all phantoms, indeed.

As you prepare to leave the hotel room, the thought of Nicanor's composition and the responsibility you feel toward that piece enters your mind. You are expected to play your part perfectly, without additional notes or idiosyncratic interpretation. You are supposed to abide by the written score. At least, that is the de facto agreement. However, you doubt Nicanor himself wants the performance to be so rigid, so limited. He came to Prague for reasons unknown to you, but he appeared at the *AghaRTA* for reasons that most likely intersect yours. There are no chance encounters in this world, and everything is orchestrated by ulterior intentions, even if you do not know what those intentions are. Nicanor must be searching for a musical dimension that goes beyond the music he committed to the score. Maybe he is looking for phantoms as well.

Heading for the *AghaRTA* is a simple matter; approaching the place, however, is more complicated. The clock in the ancient plaza tells you that high noon will happen in ten minutes. Sufficient time to get there from where you now stand. But as you embark through the narrow alley that will inevitably bring you to the *AghaRTA*, a heavy feeling takes over your body, a leaden paralysis threatens to stall your advance. This is not fear, not a fight or flight response. This is a lassitude. You want to move ahead, but your body does not respond. You wait a while, hoping to regain your normal elasticity. You take a few deep breaths. You let time and people pass you by. Another look at the clock reveals that high noon is still ten minutes away. Has time also congealed?

There you are, running around the fountain in the center of the plaza, wearing a blue summer dress, floating in the balmy air. You seem happy, unburdened, and very light. Nobody interrupts you; nobody tells you to stop. So, you continue twirling and spiraling in grace and merriment until the clock strikes that enormous bell twelve times.

At that point your body thaws and you find yourself at the door of the *AghaRTA*, standing in front of the pianist who offers you a welcoming hand.

The pianist looks like a much older man under the high noon sun. Deep recesses create shadows that crisscross his face giving the impression of a dry and desecrated territory. His smile, however, is luminous and sincere. He regards you with the same perplexity that you regard him. Perhaps he does not recognize you, or perhaps he was expecting someone else. After greeting each other, you both remain quiet in mutual observation, listening for sounds that would have accompanied either of you. Not words, those will be dealt with later. But when no sounds come into being, the pianist holds you by the elbow and begins to walk, leading you away from the *AghaRTA* into the core of the old town.

He pierces the tight and crowded streets without releasing your elbow. He walks rather slowly as if time has no meaning to him. However, his steps are certain. They have a meaning to him. You have no idea where he could be leading you, but you are not afraid. A man with such a smile can mean no harm. So, you allow him to bring you where he needs to bring you. Then, at the turn of a corner, when the noise of the crowd diminishes, you hear him humming a soft melody. It resembles the melody he was whistling last night, simple, familiar. You are content to hear it again and want to decipher the notes. But when you concentrate on the sound, it vanishes at once. Maybe you have not heard anything. It could have been an echo or a very profound wish within yourself that arises as sound.

One turn follows another, and one street leads to the next.

And there you are again, sitting in a terrace open to the breeze, playing by yourself, the sun shining shamelessly. You have been there all morning, perhaps all day, not all your life because there was another life before this one. Then your mother calls your name. You need to go inside. But you do not want to leave the breeze and the sun. Your mother calls you again. The sound of her voice is different this time, deeper, hoarser, like a sound you used to hear in that previous life. You wonder if it really is the voice of your mother. Then, a suffocating shadow, like a ghost, filters into the terrace and blocks the sun. You go inside at once.

The pianist stops in front of an old wooden door. He carefully reads the names on the brass panel next to the door and finally presses one of the little buttons. Nobody asks who is ringing, but you do hear the lock being released. He pushes the door open and ushers you inside a dark and small lobby. There he stands and looks at you as if trying to ascertain your determination to follow him. He asks if you are afraid. You are not afraid, but you wonder why he thinks that you might be. Perhaps what he is about to show you is unpleasant. Or perhaps he himself is afraid and wants to know if you share the feeling. You tell him no, that you are not afraid, but that you would like to know where he is leading you. He says that he could not tell you in words. Then he holds you tight by the elbow and starts climbing a set of stairs, every step announced by a loud and crisp crackling.

On the third floor, the second door to the right is slightly open. The pianist stops in front of it and catches his breath. The hand holding your elbow begins to shake a little. Maybe he is afraid of what he is doing, or maybe he is simply exhausted. Or perhaps he is rather excited. You cannot tell. After he calms down, he lets go of your elbow and advances through the door without knocking. You stay behind and try to listen for any voices coming from inside the apartment. There is nothing but silence. Then you hear a shuffling of steps and what appears to be a chair pushed aside, but no voices. You wait and focus on the mauve tone of the shadows that bathe the corridor where you stand. You came here by choice, persuaded by a whistle and a diffuse memory. So, what do you expect? Clarity? Certainly not clarity. Phantoms at best, or nothing at all.

What you feel is hunger. A physical desire to nourish an emaciated past so thin and incorporeal that it threatens to become extinct. What you know of your past can be reduced to rudimentary sketches of a fractured childhood plagued by inconsistencies and innumerable lies. You have considered yourself not worthy of knowledge, that whatever happened is buried in someone else's territory, that the old truths do not belong to you. Hunger, however, does not go away that easily. It needs to be satiated, rendered innocuous by aliment. There may be aliment waiting for you inside this apartment, even though the appetizer you have been served consists only of silence.

You breach the entrance and find yourself inside a rather voluminous salon where nobody is waiting for you. The decor and condition of the place sadden you. Mauve in tone as well but tinged by abandon. Joy, as well as sound, have long ago forsaken this place. At the far end of the salon, a corridor leads deeper into the belly of the apartment. It is not a particularly inviting corridor, but where else would you go in search of aliment? You forge ahead, fed by expectations. At the very end of the corridor, the faint image of your young self comes into view.

There you are, sitting on the floor, rocking back and forth while singing a sad lullaby. The rocking does not seem to soothe

Behind you a door opens slightly allowing for a sliver
of light to cut into the corridor. The light is accompanied
by the sound of a somber voice humming the same melody
the pianist whistled last night at the club. So familiar this
melody, yet so remote. You stand by the door and refrain
from pushing it open. Why interfere with the circumstances when perhaps you are about to be fed? It does not seem
the voice is that of the pianist. Its register is deeper and
carries a sadness that does not correspond to the laughter
of the pianist. The melody wants to be merry, but the voice
holds it back. She sang this melody for you. You are almost
certain. But you do not know if it was on that island of hers
or even before, in a place as dark as this corridor where the
melody would not have had the opportunity to shine.

The aliment does not sit well with you. You feel your
inners revolting and a sense of vertigo. You want to listen
to the melody and elicit the joy it promises. But the more
it resonates and the deeper it burns inside your mind, the
more desolate you feel, and the more nauseating the melody
becomes. You came here to know more and feel more, but

not to enhance your misery. So, you push the door open…

There you are… sitting on the old man's knees… listening to his song… There she is… your mother… sitting in a corner… looking dejected…

And you do not know what happens between the two of them. Why the discrepancy? Why is the memory so vague?

You turn your back on old Králová. He is still alive, something you were not counting on. The pianist moves out of the way when you run for the door. In the dark corridor the nausea overtakes you, everything inside of you rushes out. You leave with nothing inside.

#

The problem with wanting to know is that you may, in fact, get to know something. And once you have learned about something, it becomes part of your life, and there is no way of denying it. Knowledge promises power and freedom, but at the same time, it can inflict a wound on the delicate tissue of your reality. The truth, nevertheless, is that you are searching for knowledge that is suspected or partially known to you. So, when you confirm your suspicion, an emotional response ensues. But, had you not already expected such a response? Had you not already traversed the sufferance of a vision of that monster? Alive, breathing the same air as you? Yes, you have. But you had not envisioned that he would be humming a melody that incarnates some of the sweetest memories of your mother. An aberration, that is. An upheaval of the fragile mastery of your unsettled past.

The pianist knows him. How well, you know not, but well enough to have heard that melody before. The old, failed violinist and the pianist must have shared moments of intimacy when music happens without undue expectations. Perhaps the pianist has known your mother as well. And if he has, he must have seen you as a child before the calamity of the departure. But this could all be a figment of your imagination, for there is no indication the pianist really knows who you are. He did not go out looking for you. You were the one appearing at the *AghaRTA* in search of a place to express your inner music. He allowed you to play without having any idea of your purpose. You told him you were going to play nothing and everything, that is all. A rather vague proposition. Something in your playing must have impacted him. Perhaps a recognition of familiar harmonies, as he mentioned. Or perhaps a recognition of your image as a child. He did laugh, after all. However, you did mention your name.

What does Nicanor know about the pianist, about the old man? Why do you even think about Nicanor in relation to these two phantoms? Because he was sitting in the front row of the *AghaRTA*? Nicanor who probably thinks jazz is a transgression of the canon. He who composes music lacking sensible notes, betraying his own insecurities. Notwithstanding, it would be absurd to consider these encounters as pure chance. Chance amasses the souls of those who bear no affiliation to each other. Once a link exists between those souls, chance is no longer in operation. You came to Prague for a reason, and so did Nicanor. You searched an underground jazz club for a reason, and so did Nicanor. The pianist could not have expected for either of you to appear in his realm. But he was there to play his music and to listen to the music of others. He is the conduit. And the function of the conduit is to allow the flow of sounds, feelings, and memories. In essence, to foster the exchange of the souls.

You have seen more of yourself and heard more of those early melodies, but you have nothing tangible in your hands. Like submerging yourself halfway in the waters of a river, part of your body is wet and cold, the other dry and raging. The old man is alive. A disturbing fact you had not anticipated, forcing you to remember his monstrosity and the circumstances of your mother's fleeing. The harshness of that life period has remained hidden inside the obscure chambers of your inner self. The soothing balm of music has kept the rage from erupting. When you improvise, the violin notes absorb that irascible energy and turn it into harmonies the other musicians celebrate, and the audience applauds. But that is precisely what needs to be unraveled. You came to Prague to know more. You are in the midst of finding out more. Your own music, then, and the one you interpret, need to allow for the buried sentiments to show their faces and scream if necessary. Those are the missing notes.

Half of the day is already dead, but the other half is alive and promising. There is no use in ruminating about the old man, in letting dark memories cast venomous shades over timid memories. Music is the vector of illumination, which you can use to pierce through the darkness. You still have time to fathom your inner self and the effusive old town that surrounds you at this moment. But you must start somewhere. Nicanor, Nicanor… he probably knows more than he reveals. He takes shelter under a dome of aloofness and a reserved demeanor. Anyhow, he is a composer, and as such, he ought to be searching for immortality. What precludes him from touching immortality must be the subject of his search, the reason for his displacement to Prague. He cannot be following you for who you are as a person. No, he probably thinks you hold the key to understanding that which he misses. You are an instrument to him. But you first need to clarify that which you miss; you must identify your own absences. And even if it seems improbable, perhaps Nicanor could assist you in this journey.

Where to find Nicanor? Physically, he could be in a room of a shabby hotel, in the streets of the old town, walking along the river, or spying on you this very moment. Spiritually, he could be found in his compositions. Although, he is not entirely present in Composition No. 33, as you already know. Regardless, you must go after him in the same way he seems to be going after you, with intention but in an aleatoric way. That is your imperative. So, you take to the streets, that impossible entanglement traversed by a legion of people. Nicanor could be among them. But where? You do not know what draws his attention—the old façades, the open plazas, the music stores, the crowded cafés? On the other hand, he may not be attracted by any of those common elements. Indeed, if he were intent in following you, as you intuit, he would be trying to guess what draws your attention so he could track you and hopefully find you among the same legion of people.

After walking for a few minutes with no direction in mind, you arrive at a corner café from where you can easily survey the passersby. This would be a place Nicanor would likely select if he had the same purpose in mind. Thus, you are not observing the flow of people but waiting for the arrival of Nicanor himself. And since you have no obligation to survey anyone, you abandon yourself to the exercise of waiting, which is not necessarily a passive enterprise. What catches your attention immediately, is the inherent music of the town. People in the town compose this music, unknowingly, by walking, talking, hauling their pets and children, making love. You welcome the music and to better focus your attention on the melodies, you close your eyes. The sounds expand as if the town itself were an immense stage. You can identify some familiar cadences, but at its core, it remains a foreign music.

Then an abrupt noiselessness interrupts the musical interlude, as if people had arrested their walking and talking as if the town had suddenly closed its curtains. Faced with this sonic vacuum, you open your eyes…

And there, in front of the café where you are sitting, your mother walks down the street with you in tow. She is virtually dragging you as you seem resistant to follow her lead. A few meters in front of you both, the old man walks with ease, straight, not caring for what happens behind him. He is talking out loud in that language you never understood. His words sound harsh, dispossessed of paternal warmth, even brutal. You see them, you see yourself, walking all the way down the street until finally turning into a narrow alley. They are no longer there.

You are left inside the vacuum, molested by the memory, unable to truly remember what happened before or after this vision. Then the noiselessness crumbles, and the town opens its curtains again. You close your eyes and listen once more to the music of the streets. A soothing melody then reaches your ears, perhaps this one is linked to those early days. But before you have a chance to listen well, the melody breaks apart into dissonant notes and fades away.

The river of people matters little to you. They are anonymous entities that constitute the corpus of the town. Like individual notes in a symphony, their importance is relative and by no means absolute. Except for one single note that resonates loudly among the others, and that is the silhouette of Nicanor that becomes visible at a short distance from where you are sitting. He walks slowly as if he has no pressing agenda. Or perhaps his agenda is not to miss anything and to carefully identify your trace. This, of course, would be the case only if he is truly looking for you. He advances in a meticulous way, step-by-step, but undoubtedly getting closer to you. Once he is within shouting distance, you refrain from calling his name. Instead, you turn your face and body away from him, hoping he will not notice your presence. He does not. At this moment, he stops walking. He simply stands still and surveys the area for some time. Then he enters the same café where you are, sits at a table away from you, and becomes absorbed by the same flow of people that had caught your attention earlier.

You know very little about Nicanor. He is remarkably distant during rehearsals, immersed in his tightly wrapped private world. He never reveals anything about himself, neither does he ask the musicians any personal questions. His compositions are not that personal, either. Somewhere, you are sure, there must be more to him other than his unobtrusive visible self. And now there he is, sitting at a nearby table, operating out in the open, probably looking for you without knowing you are looking at him.

He carries with him a black box, which he places on the table. A sort of sound recorder, you guess, because he attaches a cable and a microphone to this box. He then props the microphone up and leans back on his chair. What is he collecting? People's voices, street noise, loose sounds, the music of the town? Why does he need to record whatever that is? You appreciate the music that emanates spontaneously from the street, but you never felt the need to capture it. That music emerges on its own and vanishes as it wishes. Why would anyone try to retain it? You would never interfere with the world during its solo.

Nicanor orders a glass of wine, which probably means he intends to sit at the café for a while. He will most likely stay until you turn up in his world. But you are already in his surroundings; he just does not know it. And no, you will not reveal your presence to him. Better to quietly observe his behaviors, for there is so much to learn from that. You are not a voyeur since you do not take pleasure or pain in observing him. You just know that he came to Prague looking for you and probably looking for something else. He already found you at the *AghaRTA*, and then he disappeared. That something else is what he is after, even if whatever that is happens to be intimately intertwined with you. So, you preserve your silence and your anonymity, and to prepare for the long wait, you order a glass of champagne, close your eyes, and lean back on your chair.

There, there, sitting on the sidewalk, still wearing that blue dress your mother says looks good on you. You are alone, but that does not bother you because you have an entire orchestra in front of you. You know the orchestra isn't there for real, but you make believe it is. With an imaginary baton in your right hand, you command the violins to play the first notes, the overture to your new life, which is soon to begin somewhere south from here. Your mother said it will be a warm place. Then your baton summons the harps and the oboes and who knows what other instruments. The entire orchestra plays your music, the music of that warm place. It is light, it smells of fresh flowers, it wants to play with you.

When the concert is over, and you open your eyes, you realize the world around you has changed slightly. The flow of people has not ebbed, and the street noises remain intact. Yet, there is nobody sitting at the table previously occupied by Nicanor. The only trace he left was an empty glass of wine.

I am starting to think that the soul of sounds cannot be recorded. I can go out in the world and try to capture the beauty of people talking or the whisper of loose winds, but in the end, all I recover is noise, a sort of sonic mud. I was there today, at a terrace café, and I am certain I heard the violins, the harp, and the oboes. Somewhere, a fragile orchestra was playing a scented and promising piece. But the recording of that piece is pure garbage, as if the music extricated its own soul, leaving behind a shameful detritus. I cannot blame the music for doing this; I would not like to be captured myself. But if such were the case at every instance, why do we bother trying to reproduce sounds? Such a soulless experience, like propping up a cadaver and trying to interact with it.

I turn off the recorder and step up to the window once more. There goes a bird flapping its wings. A song was created in that process. I cannot hear it; I cannot hold it in my hands; I cannot possess it. But that song has a soul and a reason for being. The flapping act will be repeated over and over throughout the lifetime of that bird. And its bird comrades will also be playing the same song while flapping their wings. All those songs, with their individual souls, ascend up to the heavens, where they merge with all other songs that have been produced throughout history. I cannot reach up there, but why would I want to? What I hear, I hear in the now, the soul of which communicates with my soul in the now. Once the communion has taken place, our souls separate, leaving behind a memory. Perhaps that is what memories are, the intangible detritus of the ephemeral encounters of our souls.

Neva is somewhere out there, playing her music and being herself. For a moment, during her improvisation the other night, I believe I heard traces of the fugitive melody. Of course, it could all be a figment of my imagination. I could have fabricated harmonies that she did not play at all. I could have arranged those notes in my mind, composing the very melody that escapes me. I am not certain of what she really played. I wonder if she, herself, is aware of what she plays when improvising. The notes may be simply gathering force, making aleatory alliances among themselves, then finally erupting when her bow scratches the strings. Nevertheless, those notes must be responding to an inner drive, an inner life, or perhaps to suppressed memories.

How is that process different from my own compositional efforts? What is it that I really compose? An orderly array of sounds? But if sounds lose their souls when recorded, they will also lose their souls when written down in the form of music. My compositions may be empty shells devoid of the anima that would appeal to the human mind. Or, perhaps, those compositions point in the direction of an inner life that needs to be revealed and extracted by a sensitive musician like Neva. When she played Composition No. 33, she played the notes that were not written. She could not have known what those notes were before starting to play the piece, before prying open the shell. Thus, she is a conduit, the sibyl of an oracle that does not talk to me. That would make her indispensable in my search for those notes, even if she is not conscious of what they are.

I know I can find her at the jazz club. Judging by the intensity of her playing, she must feel satisfied when improvising releases. She is clearly attracted to that sort of expression. I even wonder if she cares to play the music of dead composers or that of contemporary and pompous composers like me. Am I pompous? I do not want to be, but I cannot judge that by myself. However, if I were to follow her into the bowels of the *AghaRTA*, it would clearly be an act of irreverent pomposity on my part. So, I must find her in nature where there are no stages or egocentric musicians. Nature has no agenda of its own, it follows the rhythm of the universe and it is content with itself. I can see that from my window—the birds that just went by, the trees that swing and sway when touched by the breeze—all in perfect unison with itself. That should be the natural condition of our souls. So, the angst that suffocates me is the result of a dissonance between my natural music and that which I write on those five horizontal lines. So, I shall look for Neva in nature, and for myself in the confluence of memories.

The river is the most natural of all elements that traverse this old town. It already existed before the town came alive, and it will continue to exist once the town falls over and dies. It never stops singing, the river, and its song is pure, unadulterated. That is why people gravitate to its shore, to listen to an honest and ancient song. And that song is an improvisation, for the river does not rehearse, nor does it care for prearranged rhythms. It simply flows, and so does its music, unencumbered, organic, true to itself.

Take me to the river—take me to the flow. Down from the castle hill, I march in haste among the crowds. I do not need to know exactly where the river is. It will come to meet me; it will lie on its back, waiting for my arrival. All I need to do is descend to the lowest ground, and there it will be, flowing or singing, which is one and the same. With such certainty, I continue what could be construed as a downfall when, indeed, I am ascending to the musical excellence of nature's improvisation. And not before long, I come to the mouth of that bridge fringed by baroque statues offering me safe passage over the flowing waters. As inviting as the bridge can be, I opt out of its offer and descend further until I am confronting the river as an equal.

I know the waters of the river are never the same, thus, the river has no memory. It cannot remember me, nor could it sing for me an old song. What I seem to recognize when standing in front of it, what I draw from my own recollections, is not the current itself or the songs but the vision of the land as it bends its knee to the flowing waters. The river parts the land, and the land has no recourse but to yield and listen. And we are not different, so I bend my knee and humbly abandon myself to the song of the river.

There, there I am, lifting a river rock and looking for small shrimp. They are quiet, the shrimp, hiding from children like me, or simply crouching and waiting for prey to come their way. They say that if you taunt them with a wooden stick, the shrimp will grab the stick with their claw, then you catch them. But that is not happening. So, I go on jumping along the shore until I land on a mossy rock. Then I slide and fall in the water. It is cold. That is when I hear her. Her song vibrates loudly, like a sunken heart that wants to rise from the waters. Even when I cover my ears, I can still hear her. Yes, I hear her, but I do not want to see her because you are not supposed to. They say she is half woman and half fish. I better not look. I am not looking. How cold this water is!

People descend to the shore for various reasons, none of which have anything to do with me. I am simply expecting Neva to arrive. I do not come here to do drugs or to steal a kiss. So, I walk at a very slow pace along the shore, under the canopy of a few trees, which can attest to my sincerity. The others, those people whose reasons I ignore, walk around me speaking in an array of languages. Interestingly, there are no musicians down by the river. They like to congregate along the bridge or in the corners of the numerous plazas that populate this town. That is where they play their music, and sometimes my own music, a frightening experience that was. But I am not here to listen to any of that, and I am here to encounter the natural essence of Neva—she who may or may not have any reasons to come to the river.

While I am thinking these thoughts, I feel a hand land

on my shoulder. It is a heavy hand, the weight of which makes me slump down a little. I resist my initial impulse to slap the hand off. Instead, I let it stay in place and gradually turn around to come to know the body attached to it. I recognize the person at once. The very guitar player who sang for me a song he knew nothing about. His dog sits next to him with its nose sampling the air around my feet. They are both here, the man and his dog. And before I get to say anything, he retrieves his hand and starts speaking Spanish in an accent familiar to me. He talks about things that cannot be seen, music perhaps. He also talks about things once seen that are no longer there. What strikes me about him is his directness. He addresses me as if I were an old friend of his, as if we shared a common background. As I listen to him, I wonder what the current that connects the two of us is. It may be mere coincidence, maybe a life of music, or perhaps ancestral elements that I fail to recognize. At this moment, I cannot really tell.

I realize he does not carry the guitar with him. This saddens me, for I would have asked him to play that melody again. Yes, he said he had no idea what that melody was, but I would have asked him nonetheless. Guitar or not, I like to know more about this person who seems to know something about me, even if he is not aware of that. So, I interrupt his speech and ask why he comes down to the river. Immediately, as if propelled by an eruptive force, he begins to talk abundantly while his dog seems to nod in approval. I learn that the river is like an ocean to him, that he comes here because he misses that vast body of water, that he loves the way this river sings, that even his dog drags him here, that he cannot be himself up there in the plaza because people ask him to play songs he would rather not play, that he sees something familiar in me. All of these I take in and try to digest. Intrigued by the image of the river as an ocean, I then ask him where he is from in the least intrusive way I could muster. He says that he is from Cuba and that he came to this town as a child with his father, who has been dead for a while. Then he falls silent, and I do not know if he is listening to the song of the river or to the sound of his memories.

After a while, once he seems to return to the here and now, he asks me if I know anything about music. This simple question sends a cold arrow down my spine. I am supposed to know about music. But in this very moment, I am no longer certain that the music I compose represents who I am as a person. So, I hesitate to answer. He appears to detect my vacillation because he asks for a second time what do I know about music. I tell him I do not know a thing about music. He smiles and shakes his head. Then says that even his dog can smell that I am a musician, that the music was keeping me company when I turned that corner around the plaza, that he played the song that was already inside of me.

To avoid the music subject and the eventual exposition of my shortcomings, I make a desperate attempt to steer the conversation toward the topic of his father. That seems to touch him deeply, to the point of silencing him. Maybe he needs someone to listen. He already said he is tired of people asking him to play music that has nothing to do with him. So, I ask him why his father came to this town from such a remote island. He asks me if I really need to know that. I consider my question and try to gauge whether it is an impertinent one. I do not think so since I am searching for a common ground, that familiarity he just referred to. With confidence, I then tell him that I need to know because there are moments in life when coincidences should not be ignored. He looks at me, caresses his dog, and falls silent again. For a moment, I thought I lost him. He may not say another word or just keep walking with his dog along the river while letting my question hang in the air until it dries out. But then he looks at me again and says that his father came here to work as a mason, that the government sent him, and that he drank himself to death. After answering my question, he turns around and keeps on walking with his dog along the river.

#

The guitar player is not the reason why I came to the river, and neither is his dog. The universe cares very little for what our reasons are. Things happen, life goes on, and the fact that our paths intersect has nothing to do with any reasoning. We may share similar sensibilities, like the love for music and the appreciation of the river flow. Those

could have directed us to a common ground at the shore of
the river. But the uneasiness when we both consider our
backgrounds is entirely coincidental, unexpected, and in-
triguing. Such a visceral force should be left unmolested.
So that explains why I do not run after him. Our paths will
intersect again; it is inevitable.

On the other hand, I came to the river hoping to find
Neva in an open and natural setting, away from stage lights
and underground reverberations. Clearly, nothing guarantees that we will come across each other. Nevertheless, I
must expand the search effort since my residence at the
river shore has been rather short and has covered very little ground. I do not know what an exhaustive effort would
be, but so far, it seems inadequate to me. Thus, I meander
around while delighting myself in the games the sun and
the river play with each other.

I come to a large rock at the edge of the stream and climb
on its top. From here, I benefit from a wide view of the river. I can see how it makes its sinusoidal way between the
two land masses. The river was here before people decided
to settle on its shores. The river was the original cause, the
force that subjugated those nomadic tribes to slow down
and reconsider their ways. I understand them; I feel the
same way. I could continue searching all over the land, unbridled, with minimal confidence in finding Neva, the fugitive melody, or the past that plays tricks on me. Instead,
I could also come to the source, which is nothing but a
flow—of water, of music, of memories.

Then I think I see her. Or maybe I want to see her. A woman, most likely a total stranger, approaches from a distance. I study the movements of her body and the way she sways as she walks, but those observations reveal nothing to me. She stops her march to look at the river. She appears to be in no hurry, her eyes lost, contemplating the flowing waters and the undulating terrain. She could be singing a private melody to herself. She could also be remembering past events that seem so remote now. I do not know exactly what this stranger is doing, but I sense certain vibrations from a distance that lead me to think about Neva. If it were her, those vibrations would come to me in the form of musical notes, an improvised melody speaking about life. Regardless, this woman is at the edge of the river, perhaps at the edge of herself—or maybe that is what I want to believe.

She detaches from her contemplative self and continues to march in my direction. She moves so slowly, a gentle sway that resonates with the flow of the river.

That's me with the guitar, alone, trying to play a simple song. Using a cassette player, I record the guitar and myself singing. So stupid! I play back the recording. No, no, that cannot be... I listen again, and the mortification stabs me with violence once, twice, more... You're so miserable, you. I place the guitar on its stand with utmost care, then I run away from it. I'll never play it again.

As she approaches, I come to realize that it is indeed Neva and that those vibrations are real. However, she is unarmed. No violin case hangs from her shoulder. So, she is unable to produce music in the traditional sense. The vibrations I sense must be emanating from the core of herself, from the magma of her origin.

—Nicanor by the river... Are you going to tell me that you were not expecting to see me here?

—No, on the contrary, I came here with the full expectation of finding you. But things never turn out the way I expect them to. So, you may be correct; I doubted very much that I would find you here by the edge of the river. Nevertheless, I did come here anyway because I mistrust myself. I behave in ways that sometimes contradict my own reasoning.

—Is that the way you compose your music?

—I'm not so sure anymore how it is that I compose my music. Are you conscious of how you play your violin?

—It depends on what I'm playing. If the music is already written, I play the notes on the staff. If I'm improvising, I play from memory.

—But when you played Composition No. 33, you did not play what I wrote.

—I did play what you wrote. But I also played from memory.

—What were you remembering then?

—I don't know. Sometimes, the memories come unannounced, and I cannot know where they come from.

—But those are memories. They must originate from past experiences. Don't you think so?

—Who wants to know how things happened in the

past? Let the memories come forth if they may. In the end, they're all twisted and misconstrued. I wouldn't trust them.

—So then, you don't trust the source of your improvisations.

—Like the way you don't trust what you compose.

—That's a harsh reality. So, what's left for us?

—There's the river.

—Do you think the river remembers?

—The river remembers nothing. It knows who we are and why we come to its shore. But it doesn't care about us. It keeps on flowing like a memory that refuses to be captured.

—I've heard melodies that behave like memories.

—Yes, those you can't take captive.

She turns her back on me and continues to contemplate the river. Perhaps she is trying to pull some memories from the waters. Or perhaps she is just ignoring me. She has no need to justify her actions because she seems to be a free and determined woman. Then, she raises her arms with the grace of a ballerina and assumes the pose of a violin player. Her left hand is at eye level, and her left shoulder opened. The right hand is in front of her as if grabbing the bow. There she rests, still, while her eyes gradually close until there is nothing else to see. Then, she begins to play in the thin air. The fingers of her left hand dance over an invisible fingerboard while the right hand moves like a swan's neck, bowing undetectable strings. The fluid movements vary in cadence and speed, and her body undulates to the rhythm of the ripples on the water's surface. She is playing the music of the river or the music of her memories. My ears hear nothing, but I am completely mystified by the beauty of this soundless melody that flows through me, leaving no trace of its passage.

When she stops playing, bringing her arms down to the sides of her body, I feel as if I have been a witness to a silent miracle. She did not play for me, but she played through me. My mind believes that we are both here for a reason, that what she plays touches the ground in a land far away from here, that she could open within me a way of feeling that my memories seem reluctant to reveal. It is evident that music is not only what we hear but what our minds interpret.

I do not know what to say, so I stay quiet and watch as Neva turns toward me. With her eyes still closed, she seems to be in a state of perfect peace with herself. She does not appear emotionally affected by the music she just played. Could it be that she is utterly familiar with the source of the music, thus, it does not threaten her sense of self? Or could it be that the sole intention for her silent performance was to ignite a sense of bewilderment within me? I better stay quiet and wait for the miracle to unravel on its own. She then opens her eyes, and as if she were returning from that faraway land, she talks to me.

—That was the river singing.

—I thought it was you that I heard.

—I didn't play a single note. I only transmitted an old song the river must have learned from those who walk by.

Have you heard it before?

—I don't know exactly what I heard, but I felt as if it was meant for me.

—Could you compose a piece around that melody?

—Probably not. I cannot identify the melody.

—Neither could I because it was soundless.

—So, what did we both hear?

—Nothing and everything. That's precisely what we heard.

That may not be an evasive answer. Neva probably sees the world on those terms—a dialectical opposition encompassing all that we hear and what we do not, what she plays and does not play, the music born from her inner self and that which merely passes through her. How else could she reconcile her life as a jazz player down in subterranean clubs with her life as a string quartet player up under the rarified light of concert halls? Her sense of who she is as a musician seems to be as versatile as the changing waters of the river. Furthermore, she seems capable of coupling her memories with her current life without bleeding or shedding tears. I should learn from her.

—Tell me, Neva, why did you come to Prague just before the concert? What's here that matters to you?

—Tell me, Nicanor, why did you come to Prague just before the premiere of your composition?

—Because you came here yourself.

—But you're not looking for me exactly. I can tell.

—You're correct. I'm not looking for you, but for what

you know about me. There's that melody, those notes that revolve around you. I think that somehow, they're part of me.

—Then you should listen.

—I've been listening.

—Then listen some more.

She turns her back on me. As she slowly starts to walk away, I hope to catch a humming or a whistling containing the fleeting notes. All I hear are her steps and the river slapping on rocks at the shore.

#

Let the river sing as it wishes. Let Neva play as she must. At this moment, I need to eradicate myself from the shore and reach higher ground where I may find a stable situation. Fluidity weakens my sense of self. Even if it leads to a deeper understanding, fluidity threatens me right now. So, I walk away from the river, from the possibility of coming across those who can tune into my deep vulnerabilities. I follow the path leading back to the bridge. Once I arrive at the bridge's footing, I contemplate the structure and how it arches its back over the river, connecting one land with another. The mass of people traversing the bridge is rather impressive. I dodge them and slowly make my way until I reach what I consider to be the center of the bridge, its highest point. Here, I stop and lean over the balustrade. The river is still flowing, perhaps singing, clearly below me.

I can see the river, but the river cannot see me. I feel detached now.

I walk in the direction of the old town among the crowd, up to the edge of the land. This is solid ground to stand on. This land has been here forever and knows about other lands. Perhaps it can show me the way back to where melodies come from. Detached as I am, I begin an aimless meandering through the narrow and twisted alleys with the hope of finding something I cannot envision. It matters little to me where I go so long as the land feels solid under my feet. My mind, however, goes on a trip of its own...

There I am, entering a dreadful Soviet store where sadness is in full display. I have money in my pocket but nothing to spend it on. I go up and down the aisles and convince myself that hopelessness is the only thing for sale here. Then, I come upon a counter where a shiny harmonica awaits a buyer. By itself, the little object is nothing. But it has the power to generate music. I haven't played any instrument since that stupid guitar so long ago. It doesn't matter; I may end up doing something with music later in life. So, I use the few korunas I have left to buy the harmonica. The clerk doesn't smile when I walk away.

Every store proposes something, but nothing that serves me at this juncture. In fact, what I need right now is unclear to me. I thought what I needed most was to come across Neva out in the open world. That already happened, and here I am, walking away from her. Or, more precisely, she walked away from me. However, she presented me with something intangible in the form of soundless music. No, that cannot be touched.

The alleys turn and turn while the dark cobblestones accept my steps. I can hear myself walking, but I cannot hear myself thinking. That is probably a relief, for my inner world is in disarray at this point. Thus, I walk at the rhythm of my own steps while avoiding the tyranny of reasoning. In such a way I am gliding when a store window catches my attention and engages my abstracted mind. Behind the glass, I see a display of ancient maps from various parts of the world. These are the same lands we know today but regarded by the eyes of our ancestors. It seems they had a duty to lay out the lands of the world so others could comprehend the geographical relationships between those lands. What matters to me is that people inhabit those lands, those people make music, and music is language. So, I enter the store curious about what those lands could tell me.

The walls are covered by countries, harbors, mountains, and every possible representation of our physical universe as people have imagined it over centuries. In the center of the store an *Orbis Terrarum* shows the world as it was known in medieval times, full of distortions and aberrations. There is also a brilliant celestial map showing the classical constellations predating those from the Age of Reason where allegorical figures suggest perpetual motion. I like the concept of perpetual motion. But what catches my attention is a map entitled *Terra Firma* where the European landmasses stand out from the diffuse moiré pattern of the ocean. I find this assertion of firmness a brave one, solid, almost unyielding, precisely what I need most right now.

I leave the European continent behind and move over to the Americas. The sailing interest in those maps is evident as the coastal zones and land profiles are heavily detailed while interior landmasses are left vacant. Sailors looking for *Terra Firma* needed to take to the open sea and fend against sea creatures artistically engraved in the charts. They needed to follow currents, magnetic deviations, and winds. I am certain they brought melodies with them, which were disseminated over the new world they were colonizing. I also imagine that a great quantity of melodies must have been lost during those long trips. Not every melody would have succeeded in reaching solid ground. If a sailor died, his melody would have died with him. But that is what happened centuries ago. In more recent times, the reverse process has been just as important. Music from the Americas has reached the old European continent with far-reaching influences. How else could I be seduced by a melody I cannot touch if such melody were not a foreign one?

My eyes then stumble upon an old map of the Caribbean where a stubby Floridian peninsula points its chin southeast in the direction of the Greater Antilles. The chain of islands floats on a sea far away from here, but those lands are as solid as any other *Terra Firma* sought by any sailor at any time. The largest of the islands, Cuba, stretches like a serene alligator waiting for its prey.

Nobody sees me when I board the boat in the early morning. I soon mingle among the legal passengers, hoping to acquire anonymity, the perfect condition to travel toward the unknown. The lines tying the boat to the old port are released. A full day at sea, with no cover, no food, meandering through the deck, avoiding the crew with their white caps, white shirts, and black shoes. A long day of dodging and hiding. The night falls; it has to. Full of stars in their minds, the passengers gradually disappear into their cabins. I'm alone now, suspended on this deck, under no cover, gliding over a sea that doesn't know me. I fall asleep behind a stack of lounge chairs and dream about what will come. When the night gets bored and disinterested, the sun sneaks in and begins to shine. It has to. I grab some bread from a forgotten basket. I devour it. The passengers come out in hoards wearing colorful swimsuits. I look strange in my dark bell-bottom pants. Maybe that's why the crew stare at me. I go inside the boat's small casino where luck could be found— or lost. Three coins in my pocket are all I have. The one-arm bandit swallows the coins and spits out nothing but air. That's all I have now: air. I try to grab it, but it flows away from me. Look for shade; it is too strong, this sun. Why are they staring at me, the crew? I better move around, don't stay put, lose myself among the others, pretend that I belong to the mass of passengers that know exactly where they are going. I don't know where I'm going. An island, I guess. It doesn't matter, the unknown is what matters. I think they're coming to take me away, the crew. They find me in the shade and ask for my cabin number. I say no. 33. They know that's not true, and they do take me away and bring me to a cabin where they lock me up. The sun is still shining out there, it has to. A crew member with three black bands on the sleeve of his white shirt comes into the cabin. He's smiling. He asks, why? For the adventure, I tell him. The smile cascades down from his face. He screams at me and tells me I'll cost them money. A fine, he says. I stop listening and think of the unknown. Yes, the unknown will be out there; it has to. I feel the motion of the boat sailing, but from inside this cabin, I don't see the open water. North or South, I don't know. Then, a landing; I know because they turn off the engines, and I hear people walking down the corridors. The same man as before, with his black bands on his shirt, comes into the cabin, still bothered; I can tell because spit comes out of his mouth when he talks to me. You can't step on that land; that's not where you're going, he says. I don't know where I'm going. How can he know that that's not where I'm going if I don't know it myself? The customs agents, they are coming to take you away, he adds. No, no, no, that's not the unknown that I was thinking about. Better stay quiet, say nothing, be little, disappear. They open the door of the cabin. Go on deck but not on the land. Alone now, the regular passengers descended onto the land. I can see it, the land, but I can't touch it. Walk around, shuffle around deck. The sun is so warm it bites. It makes the crew sleepy and stupid. They stop looking at me. I'm little, I'm nothing. There's the boarding ramp, and he's dozing, the man in a white shirt with no black bands. I glide silently down the boarding ramp and alight on the land.

The alligator island seems so distant now. I never look in that direction. Perhaps because everything that took place over there is now covered by veil after veil of time, confusion, and disenchantment. We all came from there, but we went separate ways for lack of bonding. There was no music to tie the family together. Any melody sung to me in my early years is now completely forgotten. That is why I compose the music of the now and give my compositions numbers as titles. If I were to assign them names, the emotional emptiness would become all too evident.

After examining the old map, it becomes evident to me that it was drafted with the hope of communicating information between people across time. I am looking at the silhouette of the land that gave birth to my parents, and the parents of my parents. It gave birth to me as well, or so I have been told. What remains of that era is minimal, or perhaps the imprint on my neural tissue is rather thin. This map stands as the representation of the concept of land, and as such, it tantalizes my memory. I can touch the map—the concept—but I cannot touch the land.

I ask the clerk for information on the map. I am told that it is a copperplate engraving dating from the late 16th century, part of an early atlas of the New World and much sought after by collectors. But my needs and those of collectors are not the same. They care about condition, printing techniques, and buying and selling potential. I care about a land and the musical memories it may have engendered, not so much about the people and very little about material worth. However, once in my hands, the image on this map wants to merge with my rudimentary memories. The sound of my fingertips sliding over the old paper creates a sensuous melody reminiscent of the fugitive one. This is not the land of my ancestors but only an image. This is not the sound of my memories but only an evocation. Regardless, I cannot let it go. Like a collector, then, seeking after an object which seems to be missing from his personal universe, I accept to pay the quoted price to guarantee exclusive possession of the map.

Upon leaving the store, the only desire I have is to find solitude and silence. I want to listen to the whispers of my past, that unknown which allures me more and more every day. I want to touch the silhouette of the land that held those who sung to me. I want to allow for my deep inner turmoil to swirl and generate its own music. I am not afraid.

Sol

The scream does not cease to dismantle your peace. There is no point in covering your ears, for the scream resides not in the air surrounding you but within yourself. You have managed to ignore this scream for most of your life, but now that you know the old man is alive, it cannot be silenced. You wish it would stop, but at the same time, you are forced to listen to it. A force that is stronger than you because it begs for resolution. What happened when you were a child belongs to the past. But discovering that the old man is alive leaves you with no other recourse than to listen to that tortured voice that cracks when trying to sing. The melody it attempts to produce degenerates as it ascends from the depths of your memory and turns into a hoarse and horrid scream. To eradicate this scream, you would need to confront it.

You wonder what kind of life he has lived. Has he met happiness? Has he been curious about your whereabouts? Did he even consider that period of his life as important? Did he ever feel guilty for what he did? Your mother never spoke about him, not a single word. You knew he continued to exist away from the island of yours, but it was forbidden to mention his name. He grew to the size of an unspeakable monster, in your mind he did. And now you know where he is, by chance perhaps, but most likely by construction for nothing ever happens that is not somehow prearranged by our own desires.

Suspecting a liaison between you and the old man, the pianist showed you the way. Like yourself, he responded to a melodic impulse. He recognized the musical elements common to your improvisation and the melodies the old man must have thrown up in the air. He is obviously ignorant of the emotional turmoil those melodies evoke. Regardless, you do not need the pianist anymore, you can retrace your steps and find that old wooden door on your own. The problem is not how to find the monster, but what would you do or say once you are confronted with the incarnation of your fragmented memories. And perhaps more frightening, would there be music, or would there be a scream?

You need reinforcement. Going empty-handed to this encounter would be like fighting a war without artillery. You need to bring the one weapon capable of overcoming the power of disgrace—your violin. It can speak for you, extract tenderness from a rock, elicit memories that refuse to show their faces. It can be forceful yet forgiving at the same time. And that flexibility is exactly what you need because you cannot anticipate how the old man will react when confronted. Neither can you predict your bodily and mental responses to the encounter. So, you accelerate your pace and stop by the hotel where your violin is resting in peace. The front desk clerk watches as you pass by, probably wondering whether you are going back to any of the jazz clubs. He does not ask because your facial expression invites no commentary.

Armed with your violin, you part the waters of the old

town and head straight to the point of departure—the entrance to the *AghaRTA*—from there, you will follow the path taken by the pianist. You are certain you will find that old wooden door, but you are not certain the old man will be there awaiting your arrival. After a few turnarounds and false leads, you eventually arrive at a street that oozes a sense of familiarity. Here you slow down your pace and heighten your awareness. Slowly, slowly... Then you stop walking altogether and wait for recognition to arrive.

There, in your bedroom, so small that there's almost no air to breathe when he comes to sit next to you on your little bed. It's not a crib, you outgrew that a long time ago, but it's not that big either. You don't like the way he plays with you. You go and tell your mother. She cries, and you don't like that either because you would rather hear her singing. But from that moment on, she stops singing altogether, and you will not hear her again until you both arrive on that island of hers.

After studying the doors on both sides of the street, you identify the old wooden one only a few meters from where you are standing. Even if you are not afraid, your heart beats a little faster than before. Perhaps the effort of walking places a load on your heart. Or perhaps some repressed memories are boiling inside of you and throwing your organism in disarray.

Stepping up to the old door requires some conviction, trespassing it requires real determination. But you came to Prague looking for answers, and some may be looming on the third floor of this building. So, you disregard your accelerated heartbeat and shallow breathing and proceed with your quest. Since you do not know which button to press on the brass panel, you press them all. And the door opens. And you enter the lobby. And you climb the stairs up to the third floor. The second door on the right is slightly open as it was when the pianist brought you here. Maybe it is an invitation, or perhaps a capitulation. It does not matter much at this point. You enter the large space and stop to catch your breath.

Nothing. Only the mauve tone and the sense of abandonment. You stand perfectly immobile and listen for signs of life. Nothing. Deep inside you expect the resurgence of the melody you heard before in this same room. But only silence comes to your encounter. If anyone truly lives here, there is not much left of that life. Although, there is that life, the one you were not aware of, still existing in what appears to be a profound detachment which does not necessarily satisfy your need for answers. So you wait, quietly, fighting back those fragmented memories that want to land on your consciousness all at once. No, you will not let yourself be diffused. You need full integrity of mind and purpose to confront this seemingly dead specter—him, who did unto you the unthinkable.

Nothing. You move around the vast space, probing for sounds or people—nothing. There is a corridor that leads to the room where you last saw him—if it was him whom you saw. You traverse the darkness until you get to the door blocking the entrance to where his miserable life still exists. There is no melody this time, not a sound. Nothing, really nothing. And nothing can hold you back now. You know he is alive and most likely behind this door. So, you push hard, as if you were pushing a tombstone, and clear the way into this room that harbors the old man responsible for so much misery. You do not see yourself as a child sitting on his knees. You do not see yourself at all. But you do see him, sitting there, present, in bone and flesh.

Nausea wants to get the best of you. You resist; you hold your breath and swallow. This is not the time for sentimentalism, fear, or any other emotion that could derail you from your purpose. So, with firm determination, you place the case on the floor and pull out the violin. You bring it to your chin, and with the steadiest hand possible, you play a long and lamenting note on the open G string. The sound must have entered the old man's brain for he turns around and looks at you. You do not know exactly what it is that he sees, whether he recognizes you, or whether he understands what is happening. But it does not matter anymore. You continue playing the same note until the room is completely saturated by the angst embedded in the sound. Then you wait for the sound to dissipate completely, after which a dreadful silence fills the room. As you confront the old man's face, the nausea grabs your intestines and throat again. It wants to dismantle you. But no, no, you do not give in.

From the silence, from the absence of sounds, the music will emerge again. It starts by boiling a few loose notes deep inside of you. Slowly, it begins to shape itself into rudimentary melodies. You cannot hear them, but you know a transformation is happening inside of you. Then, some old memories, a mixture of good and bad ones, throw themselves into the mix. This is the magma, the original substance from where you source the notes as you improvise. Then you think you hear your mother's voice singing to you. But that gets interrupted by the sound of the old man's hoarse breathing. Then you hear the cadence of a locomotive imparting a punctuated rhythm that you detest. Now, a movement inside of you wants to acquire a form, a musical form, instead of the bodily sensations that threaten to dismantle you. You hold on to your sense of self and bring the violin to the playing position. You begin to play without knowing what you are playing. You do not attempt to create harmonic order, melodies, or what have you. However, the music that arises is not chaotic; it is not multiplicity without rhythm. On the contrary, the notes organize themselves into a gentle musical theme, unrecognizable to you but capable of attenuating the nauseous spectacle of the old man's face.

You continue playing for several hours or several minutes. You cannot tell how long. The passage of time is irrelevant because the music that emanates from you does not adhere to the laws of the metronome. This is the music of your broken memories, of your disenchantments, of your losses, of your pain, of everything that exists outside of time. And you play it loud and clear for the old man to hear. He needs to listen to your music. He needs to hear the echo of his actions. So, you play and play until the notes and the memories are totally exhausted.

The old man does not say a word, and on his face, there is no expression. To you, he is a dead old man.

#

One more night, that is all you have left before returning to your regular life where ghosts are no longer present. You already learned what you needed to know. The future will have to adapt and integrate what the present has revealed to you. Your memories will need to lengthen their shadows, like those of a cypress, and help you carve your way forward. You have nothing to fear—the music is within you. But in this very last night you must touch Nicanor's conscience, by means of words or music, and share your insights for they are relevant to him, it seems.

You last saw him by the river where he expressed a yearning for a melody that you cannot identify. He claims that such melody revolves around you. If it does, it must form part of those chords you do not think about, the ones that spring up on their own when playing extemporaneously. Those chords belong to you, but you do not control them. They are the product of your childhood tears, of your joys and fears, of your aspirations, of everything that has happened to you whether you remember it or not. They are distilled from the magma, the white center of yours full of memories that no hands can touch. If that is the melody he is yearning for, you will be incapable of writing it down on any sheet music.

Composition No. 33 comes to your mind. You try to remember what it sounds like without playing a single note. You can hear the profile of the various movements, the crescendos, the adagios. You can hear how your part weaves among that of the cello and the viola, how it battles with the second violin. You played everything and much more, yet nothing of the additional music remains in your mind. Those notes cannot be summoned, they just reveal themselves surreptitiously when your mind is at ease. And that is precisely what you ought to do: set your mind at peace and let go of all limitations, whether real or imaginary, ancient or immediate. All the constraints must be nullified, exorcized, rendered incapable of altering the music that you want to play. In other words, you want to improvise.

You could choose to go elsewhere, but it is at the *AghaR-TA* that two important events have taken place. First, Nicanor found you there, which you believe was not by accident. Second, the pianist understood what your music is all about and gave you free range to release as many notes as you thought were necessary. Plus, he recognized the melodic resemblance between your music and the humming of the old man. He is now dead to you, the old man, and maybe you ought to tell the pianist about this ontological death. Or, perhaps, all you need to do is play your music unapologetically. In essence, the *AghaRTA* is rather consequential.

But, of course, nothing guarantees that the pianist will be managing the scene tonight, nor that Nicanor will come to your encounter.

Furthermore, your playing may not emerge as resonant and expository of that island of hers. Regardless, it is to the *AghaRTA* that your path will lead this very last night. You will descend to the underground of this old town where resolution awaits you.

You see yourself picking up the violin to play what you want, not what the teacher told you. Nobody can listen to you now. Your mother is gone. Alone is better because you can cry all you want. There's that first screech of the E string, loud, cutting through the veil of that nightmare that keeps on showing up every night. Cut it with a sharp and loud sound so that it dies once and for all. Then you go hard on the G string and make it sound low, deep—like a moaning. The louder it sounds, the less you hear his whisper. You drown his deep breath with the heavy sound of the violin. Then you cry as much as you want.

Your memory had the delicacy to make you forget and remember in equal parts and dream in full. And that is what the violin does; it dreams with you and for you so that you can better elucidate the truth of your past while projecting yourself ahead, unencumbered, and free. The music—your music—is the medium that dilutes all those fulgurant vectors. It is the element that helps you coalesce all of you. It does not matter that you will have to wait several hours before you can produce yourself at the *AghaRTA*. You can wait. What matters is that you will take the opportunity to say what you need to say by means of your music. This time, you will not be drowning anyone's voice; you will be projecting yours.

You have no agency at this moment and your whereabouts are not directed by internal impulses. So, you meander, you drift, you let yourself be carried by the wind or the incline of a particular street. You feel safe, you carry the violin with you and all your music within you. And in such a wandering mode you cover some ancient ground while your mind goes on dreaming. Dreaming in full, that is. An hour or two have gone by when, unexpectedly, the distant sound of a man and his guitar grabs your attention. He is singing in Spanish, but you do not recognize the song. You follow the sound to its source—a man sitting beside a filthy dog. With guitar in hand, he produces a rather melancholic sound that makes you think he is in some kind of distress. You simply stand in front of him and continue listening to his song. You are not the only one, other people listen as well, and you wonder if they also find his singing to express a pensive sadness.

He sings about a place far removed from this old town where a warm wind caresses the white sand of a warm shore. He yearns to be there but doubts he will ever reach that shore. He then invokes the brightness of the sun, the perfume of butterfly jasmine, the sound of a gentle voice calling on him. All of this he sings in Spanish, and you understand what he says perfectly well. However, that does not mean you understand him as a person, that is a higher order function. People around you seem to enjoy his singing and playing for they clap vigorously when he ends the song. He bows in acceptance. He then notices you and your violin case and asks if you want to join him for the next song.

There you are, wearing that blue dress your mother likes, sitting in the middle of the living room surrounded by people who call themselves your family. You know only half of your family; the other half you never speak about, your mother won't let you. And they tell you to play something. You don't want to play anything; all you want is to disappear. But you haven't learned how to disappear yet. When you grab the violin, you feel the weight of all those inquisitory eyes come crashing down on you. The enormous pressure squeezes the air out of you. They tell you to play Bach. No, not Bach; too many notes. Anything else but Bach. They ask for Bach again. You want to please them, but when you try to move your bow, your arm doesn't respond. Nobody is aware that you want to cry, and you won't let them know. You tell them you will play something. And that's what you do; you play something, but nobody knows what that is. Only you know, and you won't tell them.

He does not need you. He seems to be doing perfectly well with his guitar and his dog. If you were to join him, whatever you two would play would not be a song of his any longer. It would become a twisted melody with no clear meaning. His memories are his own, and yours belong only to you. There is no point in superimposing remembrances that are already known to everyone. It is different with Nicanor; he does not know the meaning of his memories, or so it seems. So, you walk away from an invitation that feels more like an imposition. Even if the music this man and dog play originates from that island of hers, it is better for you not to get tangled in a musical situation where you are expected to play in a certain way. What you need most is to let go of all controls and filters and release your music. In the right place, that is, where the notes have a chance to alter the current of people's lives, even if they are not aware of it. So, your meandering continues unabated for a century or so until you come to a solitary square guarded by old stone buildings. People seem not to favor this place, or perhaps it is only a forgotten square among many others. But you find it inviting due to its emptiness. Content to be here: You pull the violin out of its case and consider playing for nobody. This would only be a release of superficial notes, not the ones buried deep inside your mysterious density, which require a different kind of abandonment—a light rehearsal, you envision, of what will happen later.

Weightless as they are, the first few notes fly away without effort. And that makes you feel at ease, free, and unencumbered. You are not trying to play anything in particular; you are just happy to emulate the sound of the breeze. Your musical mind is not fully engaged at this moment, neither are your memories. Thus, your breathing is effortless, and your thoughts are transparent. Whether there is any meaning in what you are playing matters little to you. The notes simply jump out and frolic with each other in an imprecise and liberal fashion. You feel like the joyful girl you were when nothing was expected from you, when nothing was remembered by you. And this blissful moment would have continued for another century or so if it were not for the two or three people that invaded the previously empty square and throw a few coins inside the violin case.

The spell is broken, and you carry on with your meandering steps, which turn, little by little, into a march, clearly bringing you closer to the *AghaRTA*. It feels like fate even though you do not accept such strict armatures. However, you find comfort in knowing that you will arrive at your destination in an aleatory fashion, like a well-improvised musical piece that knows to land on the root note. As the streets narrow and your pulse accelerates, you know you are close to the end of your march. Step by step, you begin to slow down your tempo until you find yourself in front of the *AghaRTA*, the root note. You did not know this place existed before coming to Prague. Buried under the streets of the old town, this place allows you to play what is buried inside of you. You did not know the old man was still alive before you came to Prague, either. But he is now dead to you. You have buried him, and in so doing, you eradicated him from your memories. Tonight, your music will be completely free.

There is no point in returning to the concert hall until I have opened the door to all the music that has traversed my soul throughout all instances in my life. Perhaps that is a tall order, but not entirely ridiculous. In the end, I am the product of the events that have impacted my life, even if I do not remember all of them. I come to realize that nothing is ever destroyed inside the dark halls of our memory. Some events may be shy and quiet, but given the opportunity to express themselves, they will sing their song. The problem is that I do not exactly know what it is that I cannot remember. And not knowing has been a strait jacket in my compositions. I always felt I needed to have command of every single note and that every musical expression needs a reason to enter a composition. I have ignored what I do not know. Consequently, I have stifled my creativity. This is precisely what Neva does not do. It appears that she is comfortable not knowing what she is about to play, and because of that, she plays everything. She finds the finished written work stifling, like Composition No. 33, because that composition is hermetic and does not include the unknown. But somehow, she intuits the nature of that unknown and expresses it beautifully through her violin.

Neva told me to listen some more. I thought I made an honest effort to listen to all available sounds with the help of my sound recorder. But the truth is that those are the sounds of nature, of the physical universe. The recorder is useless when it comes to capturing the sounds of the mind. It appears that those sounds are only available to the courageous souls who do not filter their memories. I have not filtered my memories, perhaps not consciously, but I have not opened the floodgates either. So, I need to listen, listen to everything that threatens to emerge from deep inside myself, even if it is a dissonant sound.

I unroll the ancient map and begin to analyze every single line composing the shape of the alligator island. The hand of the engraver was rather firm. Cornelis van Wytfliet was his name, a geographer and musician from the Netherlands. I wonder what music he heard inside his mind while carving the copperplate around 1597. Did he have direct knowledge of the songs the creoles chanted at that time? It appears to me that he did not leave anything to chance. So, I trace the engraved lines with my finger in search of patterns, rhythms, or any indication of a melodious composition. A musical score must be embedded in this compilation of parallel and sinusoidal lines. However, I do not identify anything that would come close to a composition. It all strikes me as noise.

Perhaps the problem is that I unconsciously resist the sounds that relate to a particular time of my life. I may be deaf to certain tones and harmonies that, if allowed to resonate, would stir complicated feelings. But how would I ever know what those harmonies are if my mind deprives me from their perception? Could I trick myself into believing those are harmless notes? Perhaps I could, but to mount such an effort, I would first need to identify the threatening notes a fraction of a second before my unconscious mind has a chance to intervene. In other words, I would have to operate from silence, the virtual absence of music, the space that exists before a single note is heard. I must be naïve, uninitiated, clean of any previous perception to approach such threatening notes. Indeed, those times the fugitive melody has come to grace my reality, it has always done so when I am disarmed, expecting nothing, essentially open to everything.

I wonder what sort of music would emerge if a score were not to dictate but only to suggest the notes to be played. In the spirit of being open to everything, such a score would allow for unlimited variations responding to the idiosyncratic nature of the musicians at each performance. Every performance would express a uniqueness of its own. But at their core, all performances would retain a common original element. The composer, that is, who would exist as a sort of stem cell for the composition, like a distant relative looking at you from a faded photograph. And perhaps my shortcoming has been to insist on the ultimate necessity of every note without allowing for the possibility of variations. Such an insistence on accuracy must be the result of fear, for I quiver when a resonance goes astray or when a memory is rattled.

Considering that Composition No. 33 is to be performed within the next couple of days, I better gain understanding of what is at the core of such work so I can release it from my mind and accept the potential variations Neva would impart to the score. I should give her permission to play her part as she wishes. That is only natural, and it would be idiotic on my part to do otherwise. But what lies at the core of that composition remains elusive to me. I am not aware of everything that may have contributed to my selection of notes, harmonies, and structure of the composition. I know, for sure, that there are important elements I do not know. Those elements are showing their faces, but I am hesitant to look in their direction.

There, there I am, shirtless, playing with a ball that bounces beyond my reach. I run after the ball, but the ball keeps on bouncing away from me. I cannot reach it. I turn around, bothered, hoping that nobody saw me losing the ball. That is the only ball I have, and nobody will give me another. A woman I don't know sees me looking down at the ground. I fear she will ask me about the ball. But she doesn't. She asks me how come I don't wear a shirt. I tell her I don't have one.

If Neva is going to perform at the premier of my composition, she would need to leave Prague tomorrow at the latest, and so will I. She has not mentioned a desire to forfeit the concert. The truth is that she has not mentioned much other than tangential allusions to my need for listening. Regardless, I assume this will be her last night in this old town. I truly wonder what motivated her to come here. What is she really looking for? She turned the question around when I asked her, cleverly recognizing that I have deeper doubts of my own. I get the impression that we have both embarked on parallel paths searching for answers, one next to the other, but with different purposes in mind. However, those paths have crossed each other and produced some wonderful and ephemeral music. I must cross her path again before she vanishes tomorrow, before she tackles Composition No. 33.

I suspect she will be looking for freedom tonight. Musical freedom, that is. As for the rest of her life, I have very little knowledge. She may be facing personal constraints that I ignore. But if music is at the core of her existence, as I believe, she will be aiming to express herself as freely as possible tonight. She needs all that jazz and the space it provides. She needs to exist in that rarified expanse between musical notes. Perhaps I have the same need but have not allowed myself to recognize it. She suggested that I listen some more. And she may be correct. I should listen to all those notes I may have brushed aside, to the reverberation of my blood vessels, to the echoes of my memories, and in particular to her improvisations on the violin. That will only happen at the *AghaRTA,* where she will most likely be looking for freedom tonight. And so will I.

#

I am not a dead composer yet. So probably a few people would miss me if I were to skip the premier of my own composition. But people have no right to know my whereabouts, nor could they demand my physical presence at the concert. After all, what would my warm body do to enhance the music beyond what is already written? I am not a performer like Neva who can infuse the composition with her personal touch, even to the point of augmenting and enriching the score. All I can really provide is a sense of authenticity. I am the composer, I am alive, and I am present while my very composition is being performed. It may feel extremely real to the audience, but that has nothing to do with the musical qualities of the composition, if indeed it has any. Plus, aware of my self-critical tendencies, I will be judging how the audience responds to the music. I will be linking the duration of the applause to the inherent qualities of the piece, which, from experience, I know is completely absurd.

I am a living composer, and life is what I should be looking for. And life has no value unless it contains a decent amount of freedom. And freedom could only be savored if I am at peace with my own self. And I would only experience such peace when I finally decipher the nature of that delicate and fugitive melody. And the only person that seems capable of extracting that melody from its source is Neva. And I will not see Neva the day after tomorrow because, as I have already reasoned, I am useless at the concert, and my presence may even be deleterious to how I value my own music. Thus, I will not make a physical appearance at the concert hall. Where shall I be instead is an open question that I have no obligation to answer at this point. The only thing that is evident to me is that I must encounter Neva tonight.

As I am preparing to embark on my quest for enlightenment, an utterly disturbing thought crosses my mind. What if Neva does not show up at the jazz club tonight? What if she has already left this old town? I have a phone number that may belong her, but it would be preposterous of me to use it. Furthermore, she has no obligation to assist in my personal search for any melody that seems to be lacking in my life. She probably thinks that, as a composer, I must have all the musical answers at the tip of my fingers. I probably mean very little to her on a personal level. Whether she respects my music, that is a mystery to me. Sure, she agrees to perform the compositions, but at the end she is being paid for doing so.

Why am I immersed in so many doubts? Should I not be level-headed, confident, self-assured? Perhaps I should, since that is what others expect of creative individuals like me. But do I really create anything? Those scores I compose are only an arrangement of notes over time. What is so unique about that? Birds also sing their own compositions by arranging notes over time. They do it so well that composers try to emulate them. And those birds have no capacity for memory. Or do they? I better stop myself right now, otherwise I will keep on doubting all evening.

Maybe I am just afraid. Afraid of the periods of my life I cannot recall, of the people that may have known me and of which I have no recollection, of the sadness of having left one place after another, always leaving and always arriving, of the music that could reveal a tenderness I resist, of having to acknowledge I have a past to which I owe a great deal. Maybe I am afraid of all that and even much more that I am not aware of. But what is fear other than a preoccupation about what has yet to happen. Of course, there is the fear that nothing, indeed, may happen.

I must take to the street and take my chances. But I am not going empty-handed. I roll back the ancient map and slide it carefully inside my briefcase. Armed in such a way, I head for Wenceslas Square, where, according to my memory, I met the Cuban masons a long time ago. I do not expect to find their ghosts, but I would like to identify the café where our exchange took place. The vision of the actual place could elicit auditory sensations, which may help me unearth forgotten melodies. Those masons could have sung traditional melodies to me. I just do not remember.

Once I arrive at the square, the multitude of people and vehicles produce a raging roar that terrifies me. I endure the torture and walk up and down the sidewalk in search of familiar elements that could identify the café. There are numerous establishments, but none are recognizable to me. The images that surround me are of this time, different from those in the times of the Cubans.

But there, there, I am holding his hand on the way to the cockfighting ring. He says that I'm old enough to watch the fights. He then takes a cigar and puts it inside my shirt pocket. "You keep it there, and when I ask for it, you give it to me. You're a big boy now." That's what he says. I'm so proud to walk around with the cigar in my shirt pocket. People look at me and smile. He walks inside the ring and puts one bird in front of the other. I love their bright colors. Then the birds go crazy. I don't know why they want to kill each other. One is bleeding from the eye. I run away.

I am looking outside of myself. I better forget this useless search for visual memories when the real questions reside inside of me. Wenceslas Square will not provide me with anything other than an excuse to delay the real encounter with my fears. Yes, I should run away, but not from my fears. So, I turn around and abandon the fabled square. It served its purpose in the times of the Cubans, but this is my time now. I walk directly into the heart of the old town and follow the narrow alleys, hoping to find my way. Somehow, I sense this is the beginning of a journey I had not expected to undertake. If coming to Prague was instinctual and benign, leaving Prague may become earth-shattering and consequential. I can feel the land trembling under my feet.

At every turn, corner, and doorstep, I see the image of my young self looking at me. I recognize myself, but I am not sure my young self recognizes me, for his eyes—my eyes—stare at me as if surprised or perplexed...

I am a stranger to my own self. Or at least, in those times, I would have never imagined what I would become many years later. Sadly, when many years later have already elapsed, I cannot remember what my young self was dreaming of.

As I keep on walking deeper and deeper into the old town, the alleys take control of my compass and lead me to a place I recognize. There, further down on the right side, I see the luminous sign that reads *AghaRTA*. This is where I will descend in search for freedom. And if destiny so desires, Neva will be down there as well. And if I dare to investigate those obscure rooms of my memory, perhaps I will see my young self singing a song.

With high expectations, I dive once more into the bowels of the old town. The place is already full of people who talk to each other, smile, drink, and probably expect to hear something that will affect them. Whether that arrives by means of music or alcoholic enlightenment, I know not. In reality, these people are not different from me. Our desires may diverge. Nevertheless, we are all hunters of the underground. There is a piano and a drum kit on the stage, but no musicians yet. I look around for any announcement indicating who the players will be. There is no sign anywhere. Maybe people do not necessarily care for who the musicians will be if they are provided with the impact they desire. I move among the people and act as if I were one of them. It takes me very little time to realize that I am one of them. I must assume that, occasionally, they also see images of themselves that they do not understand. Likewise, they must be failing to ambush old fugitive melodies.

I do not need to hide tonight. I came here with intention and purpose. Let the currents flow through me, let the memories shake my foundations, let the music take me where it will. There is nothing to fear. And if my presence has an impact on Neva, it would only be reciprocal, for she has already impacted me. So, I take a highchair at the center of the bar counter from where I can survey the stage and the audience. When the bartender comes my way, I order a glass of wine and ask him who will be playing tonight. He says he does not know and that, in reality, it does not matter. He may be correct—a solid truth hides behind those words.

Time goes by. I know because I already finished the glass of wine. However, no music has eventuated. All I hear is the cumulative sound of all the expectations around me and within me. The bartender, attentive it seems, refills my glass of wine. What sort of wine he serves me I know not, but it does not matter. So, time keeps on passing by until the moment the musicians emerge from the crowd and take their places on the stage. They are not different from the audience; they just serve as conduit for their expectations. But the most important conduit, the one that fathoms the notes missing from my composition, is not among them. I thought Neva would be looking for freedom tonight. But perhaps she has taken the freedom not to appear at all. I cannot tell.

The trio embarks on an uncertain musical journey. To no avail, I try to identify what the antecedents for their arrangements are. Nothing I can clearly identify. They seem to be pirouetting around various themes, personal themes maybe. What is clear to me is that they are playing what they want to play. I detect no coercion or duress in their playing. They seem to be free, taking their solos as they see fit, respecting each other's musical ideas, reverberating individually but also as a trio. Whatever they are playing has not been written down anywhere. They may be interpreting their sorrows, their joys, perhaps their memories, and certainly their dreams. And it becomes obvious to me that the audience, myself included since I already acknowledged that I am one of them, has not come here to listen to a particular melody or composition. They are here to witness the miracle of playing, to listen as the musicians express what is inside their white center. It is the sharing of a life by means of musical notes they are after, the depuration of a soul that they expect. Like the fragrance of a rose when it opens, music emanates from them. To be experienced but not to be captured.

At some point after my third glass of wine the musicians stop playing and announce they will be taking a short pause. I feel the urge to approach them and ask about Neva. Is she arriving? Will she be playing tonight? But no, I should not pose any questions. I should let the night advance as it wishes. Let the events play out naturally, without a score, extemporaneously. The musicians descend from the stage and merge with the audience. How different from the antics of the concert halls up on the surface of the land where musicians keep the public at a distance for fear of tarnishing their musical genius. I step away from the bar and join the crowd. I do not talk to anyone, I just listen…

There now, I see myself sitting in the center of an interior patio. So small I am. I'm singing a song, but I can't hear what it sounds like. I get up and move around the patio. There's a tall wall with deep cracks on one side of the patio and a row of yellow ocher columns on the other. I'm inside this patio, alone, where nobody else comes in… and I'm singing.

People return to their places and the expectation returns to the atmosphere of the underground cave. I return to my chair at the bar and the bartender refills my glass. The musicians extract themselves from the audience. When they take the stage, I realize the trio is now a quartet. Neva has taken the freedom to join them.

When the pianist sees you arriving with your violin, he laughs that laughter of his. He does not know how it ended between you and the old man. He could not have imagined what that encounter meant to you. He just made a musical association—which was a correct one—but that was all. You have transcended the mortifying experience of that encounter. What needed to be buried is now buried. So, you accept his laughter, for it is genuine and heartfelt. When he asks you what you would like to play tonight, you say that you would like to play the "everything" part, not the "nothing" part. He laughs so hard that you fear he is going to fall over.

You take advantage of the musical pause before the second set and make it to the corner of the bar. A glass of champagne is in order because of the freedom it represents. Bubbles swim around in the golden liquid in a perfectly improvised fashion. A continuous movement not orchestrated by anyone. And like musical notes, they ascend until they exhaust themselves and join the air above. That is the "everything" you want to play tonight—the joyous amalgam of notes spiraling inside you, looking for a way to join the universe of loose notes floating in the air.

You are not obligated to be here. You are not obligated to play a single note. You are not obligated to read any sheet music. You are free to commune with your violin and the other instruments and resonate as you wish. Perhaps this is what you were doing when you played the missing notes from Composition No. 33. You were simply responding to the sentiments of people and instruments around you. There was no agency on your part, only an answer. Should not all music be approached in such a fashion? Maybe there is no answer to that question, but that is how you will play tonight.

Once on the stage, you feel a tingling sensation all over your body; something in the air touches you. You do not know what it is, but your body can feel it. Perhaps the electrical charges of so many sentiments projected unto you by the audience. You want to acknowledge them all. You want to aggregate that energy to your own. That is part of the "everything" of the contiguity of desires. When you look at the faces in the audience to identify the origin of so many desires, what you see is an immense blur. Although, one face does stand out from the rest, a face you recognize. There he is, Nicanor, sitting at the bar, looking your way, projecting his own sentiments onto you. You have felt those sentiments before, and your playing has already responded to them. All the better, he is back to listen some more, as you suggested.

The pianist sits at his bench, the drummer grabs on to his mallets, and the sax player takes a hold of the goose neck. Everyone seems ready to launch the next set. But there has been no agreement, plan, or strategy, as to what to play, what mood to pursue, or what rhythms to favor. You intuit immediately that this is not happening by mere chance. The pianist knows what he is doing. He has a sense for the needs of others. He wants you to jump into the white center of yours and lead the ensemble. And that is precisely what you do.

What follows is music, an unexpected array of harmonies that traverse the souls of everyone in the audience. It matters not what you or everyone else in the ensemble is playing. What counts is the fact that all of you are playing. Your cumulative inner world is being revealed by means of your instruments, and in the process, the cumulative inner world of the audience is being touched. That is the miracle.

However, your private miracle is a different one. In your mind's eye, images of your youth parade one after the next. Some are bright and clear, while others are more obscure, to the point of vanishing into the shadows of the cave. There is a river, and there is a sea. There is a gentle hand, and there is a hand not so gentle. A few images are full of joy, while others exude a sullen sadness. Some images make no sense to you, strange situations and people that you cannot recognize. Then, there are the images of the old man, which align with the flat notes of the violin. You play differently, then. And all these images turn around you, invisible to anyone else but rather evident to you. Interestingly, every moment a song ends, and you silence your violin, the images melt away. But as the musical miracle takes flight once more, they begin to encircle you anew.

The audience seems ecstatic about your playing. They clap, whistle, and urge you on. The pianist laughs to himself. The drummer and the sax player follow you closely and respond to your musical somersaults. But the truth is that you do not really know what you are playing. You are sourcing notes from images, images from memories, and memories from who knows what room inside your mind. What people are listening to is the depuration of your soul, the essence of who you have been and who you are. They do not know about the old man or about that island of hers, but it does not matter. What matters is that you are free to play as you wish, regardless of what may or may not have happened before. This is the unwritten music of life.

You know the second set has come to an end because the pianist stands up and starts clapping along with the audience. You would have easily continued playing since the deep well of notes is by no means empty, on the contrary, the abundance of images and the music they engender seems infinite. It does not matter; there will be a third set, or maybe the music will go on until there is nothing else to say or until all the images recede from view. Some of the spotlights in the cave shine on you, but what feels more brilliant is the multitude of eyes that regard you at this very moment. The audience has communed with you. They have listened to the music of your life in its raw state, unwritten, unchartered, born from the good and the bad, the remembered and the forgotten—the miracle of music.

You set the violin aside and let it rest until the next set. Then you descend from the stage and make your way thru the crowd to the center of the bar where Nicanor seems to be waiting for you. You stand in front of him and say nothing. His face radiates a dim light, like that of a child who fears a lonely night. He looks at you in a strange way, different from that in the concert hall during rehearsals. A sad way perhaps, but with a hint of yearning. You wonder whether he is listening to your music or that of his own life.

Do

The music has advanced as it wishes. It has found a conduit in Neva who played with abandon what appears to be a personal recital of her life. I cannot imagine what the sources of the harmonic miracle are but is clear to me that her life story inspired her playing. Her inner voice, as expressed by her violin, has both gentleness and clarity. So, to get to authenticity, she really keeps going down to the bone, to the honesty and inevitability of something. I think she has found freedom.

As she stands in front of me in icy silence, I want to tell her that she has touched me, that her music reverberates inside of me, that upon listening to her, I see images of myself as a child, singing, that I am now forced to question whether I have been honest in my compositions. I wish I could say all of this, but no words come out of my mouth. I need music now, my own. Maybe I should go down to the bone and look for whatever honest notes lie within me. But, in those hollow rooms, all I hear is silence. In Neva's icy presence, there are no melodies, only the memory of having heard them. In desperation, I reach for the briefcase and pull out the rolled ancient map. My hands tremble, not out of fear but out of anticipation. I clear away the wine glasses from the bar counter and make room for the map. I unroll the copperplate representation of my confused past. I say nothing; I just look at Neva.

—Oh, that island of hers. So far away from here. I wish... No, I don't wish.

—What do you wish?

—I don't want to wish for anything right now. I'm content as I am. How about yourself, what do you wish?

—I wish I could listen to the music of my past.

—You don't have to wish for that. It's always there. All you must do is listen.

—Yes, I can hear you playing your past music, but when I listen for my own, all I hear is silence.

—Then fill the silence, sing something.

—I think I've done that before when I was a child.

—You don't sing anymore?

—No, I only gather the notes around me and compose with them.

—Then go back to where you came from; the music will be there.

—Perhaps I should. Take a close look at this old map. Can you identify any music on this map?

—I can see all the beautiful notes, and I can hear them as well. Just follow the contours of the island, the shape of the mountains, the indentations of the rivers, the undulations of the sea. All the notes are there; nothing is missing.

I believe what she says is true. But the alligator island is a formidable blur in the confines of my memory, and as such, it elicits no sound. If I am to continue existing as a composer, I must find those sounds, the sounds of my origin, the unwritten music of life.

—Neva, I need your help. Could you play all the missing notes at the premier of Composition No. 33? You have my permission to play as you wish. I hope you do because I won't be there to listen.

—Where would you be instead?

—Far away from all of this but not from myself. Where I could stir complicated feelings, open the floodgates of my memories, listen to all possible musical variations, look in the direction of the unknown. Neva, I'm going to that island of mine. There's a melody waiting for me over there.

* * *